"Who are you?" s

"You took the words ____
replied brusquely. And why didn't she have a shrill
and squeaky voice instead of that husky contralto,
which made him long for her to whisper things a
scarred lord and mysterious lady housebreaker
could never say to one another?

"Ah, then *you* are Lord Lathbury?" she said severely.

"Am I?" he said, his old delight in the ridiculous
waking up and stretching, but he told it to go
back to sleep. "Not a difficult deduction, given my
infirmities," he said with an impatient gesture at his
damaged face. "And you have the advantage of
me, madam."

"Oh, that," she said, as if she hardly thought his
marred face worth a second glance. It must be a
clever lie, unless she was terribly shortsighted and
too vain to wear spectacles. He doubted it as she
surveyed him like an empress displeased with a
shabby courtier. "I am Melissa Aldercombe,"
she admitted stiffly.

Author Note

Of course, my books are always meant for you, but this one is dedicated to you, as well. It is a privilege to share the few precious hours you have to read and escape your busy lives. I hope this is a good enough story to help you forget the difficult times we have all been living through lately. If it helps, I am so glad and, as always, thank you for reading my books. I love what I do, but I certainly can't do it without you!

Melissa and Adam are hurt and lonely people who think they are done with love, but it certainly isn't done with them. It is so hard for them to be vulnerable to being hurt again, but they risk it anyway and somehow that made them extra special to me. I do hope you enjoy their love story as much as I enjoyed writing about them, and thank you again for being my lovely readers.

ELIZABETH BEACON

—

Falling for the Scandalous Lady

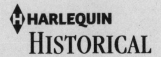

HARLEQUIN

HISTORICAL

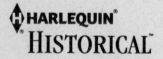

HARLEQUIN®
HISTORICAL™

ISBN-13: 978-1-335-40757-3

Falling for the Scandalous Lady

Copyright © 2021 by Elizabeth Beacon

Harlequin Enterprises ULC
22 Adelaide St. West, 41st Floor
Toronto, Ontario M5H 4E3, Canada
www.Harlequin.com

Printed in U.S.A.

Elizabeth Beacon has a passion for history and storytelling and, with the English West Country on her doorstep, never lacks a glorious setting for her books. Elizabeth tried horticulture, higher education as a mature student, briefly taught English and worked in an office before finally turning her daydreams about dashing piratical heroes and their stubborn and independent heroines into her dream job: writing Regency romances for Harlequin Historical.

Visit the Author Profile page
at Harlequin.com for more titles.

To all my lovely readers,
you are always my inspiration and thank you
for letting me do this wonderful job!

Chapter One

'What a coxcomb!' Lady Melissa Aldercombe exclaimed at the breakfast table.

'Hmm? Oh, your cousin. What's he done now?' asked the Duke of Wiston.

Melissa reread her cousin Vernon's unpleasant letter. 'Sent me this,' she said and passed her father a draft drawn on Vernon Granger's bank.

'Well, he did put you out of his dower house with indecent haste after your grandmother died; maybe it's a cockeyed way of saying sorry.'

'No, he has sold Grandmama Granger's books and papers at auction.'

'What? No, he can't have; they were left to you. I witnessed the will.'

'Apparently I might have used her notebooks and library to ape her unnatural example and publish a book of my own, so he decided to save me from myself.'

'Save him feeling a fool next to another clever female relative, more like, but we can always buy more books if that's what you want to do.'

'Do?' Melissa said as fear began to overcome rage and her hand shook so badly she put down the letter and stared unseeingly at her half-eaten breakfast.

'Write a book.'

'No, I don't have Grandmama's gift for making obscure and complex things crystal clear,' she said absently.

'Well, then, it was wrong and illegal, but I can't see a way to undo what's been done, and he has sent the proceeds.'

'You don't understand, Papa, but why would you?' Melissa said and felt guilty about keeping him on the outside yet again. Even when her father had persuaded her to make the most painful decision of her life, she knew that he had thought it was the right thing to do. But deep down perhaps she still blamed him for her having to make it. She should be adult enough to have got over his part in that terrible dilemma by now.

'After she lost her speech from the apoplexy Grandmama Granger struggled so hard to warn me there would be a scandal if those books are not kept safe.'

The Duke paled as the possible nature of that scandal hit like a blow. 'What did Mrs Granger say?' he asked with all his attention on his daughter now.

'In private, Papa,' she murmured after Carnforth, the butler, glided in with fresh coffee and the news a despatch box had arrived for the Duke.

'Aye,' he agreed with Melissa and dismissed that

important red box with an impatient gesture. They got up and left the room.

'Well?' he asked her when they were inside his very private study with the door closed on the world. 'What did she say?'

'Just a few words: *"Melissa, find, letter, mother, and son, with, my, book"*. But it was enough to make me memorise them and burn the paper they were written on. I must find that letter before anyone else can read it, Papa.'

'What possessed her to keep anything you wrote back then?'

'I truly cannot imagine,' Melissa said with a sigh for that clever and apparently also foolish woman she had loved so much. 'But I must find the letter before anyone else does.'

'Yes, but you had best leave it to me,' he said with a heavy sigh as the thought of her wild impulses of old caught them both up in a memory of the past that hurt so much she could hardly endure revisiting it, let alone knowing it could be discussed over the teacups of Mayfair as the *ton* thrilled to the truth of her downfall and the secret that the poor, dear Duke had been forced to keep because his only child was an ungovernable hoyden who had tested every rule in the book until it screamed for mercy.

'No, you can't do it, Papa. A minister in His Majesty's Government can't do whatever it takes to get those books back. People will wonder why they are so important and ferret through them to find out why you want them.'

'I don't see how you can do it without attracting attention either. The polite world is so curious about you, especially now you are living here with me again and still determined not to take your rightful place in society. I sometimes wonder if they will break in to see my elusive daughter now you are home at last and still being elusive.'

'Ugh! What a horrible notion.'

'Indeed,' he said, and it was all the things he didn't say that made her feel so guilty about putting him through even more trouble than she had already.

'I will get Grandmama's things back without anyone knowing how badly I want them somehow,' Melissa said as lightly as she could manage when her hands were clenched so hard her nails were biting into her flesh.

'I could resign from the Government.'

'No, you are needed; only think how narrow-minded and hysterical they would be without you. Let me try to get my letter back before you do anything drastic.'

It took some coaxing and persuading, but eventually the Duke agreed and Melissa knew she must never let him realise the very thought of the scandalmongers ripping her life apart if that letter ever came to light made her blood run cold.

Nearly a week later Melissa slipped inside Lord Lathbury's library and closed the door behind her, glad to have got this far undetected. There was so much flurry and fluster behind the scenes at Lathbury House tonight she had managed to slip in through the back door. She had tiptoed past the kitchens while the cook and her minions were busy and everyone else was upstairs laying out the supper room and making sure last-minute disasters were seen and dealt with. Just as well they didn't know she could be one of them if she was found at Miss Lathbury's come-out ball without an invitation.

All the old rumours about wild and ungovernable Lady Melissa Aldercombe would start again with thrilling new ones added, so she had better not be caught. At least she was in the grand part of the house now and none of the servants would bother a fashionably dressed lady flitting about His Lordship's town house on such a night. She allowed herself a brief sigh of relief and blessed Papa for insisting on ordering her a brand-new wardrobe despite her refusal to join the *ton* since he still had to look at her. Apparently it was painful when the country dressmaker she had used in Shropshire might have heard of fashion, but clearly didn't hold with it.

Never mind her appearance, although it was oddly satisfying to dress in the first stare of fashion for the first time in her adult life. It was peaceful in here and she was reminded of the atmosphere in her grandmother's humbler book room. Grief for the eccentric, determined and generous-hearted lady hit once again, but she pushed it aside and reminded herself why she was here and that it was time to concentrate on the living.

She frowned at Lord Lathbury's crammed bookshelves—finding anything here would be like searching for a needle in a haystack. So, where did the man keep any new additions to his fine collection, then? She clicked her tongue impatiently at the poor job a single candle was making of lighting the room. It was meant to say *This is private. Stray guests, please recall your manners and go back to the ballroom.*

She lit a branch of them and ignored it, hoping His Lordship's staff would think an intrusive guest had stolen in here for a tryst with a lover when they found them tomorrow. No doubt they would curse the careless ways of the *ton* and replace them before the master of the house left his bed. Nobody would know she was here and this was her chance to search for her letter while the man was hosting his sister's debut ball. She headed for the piles of books and papers on the library table and tried not to feel guilty about invading his privacy.

The idea of a stranger reading her own hasty words, written at the most terrible and wonderful time of her life, made her shudder, though, so never mind His Lordship's privacy—she had to find that letter. Although she had changed drastically after her son was born, she would still dare anything to keep him safe.

She had forced herself to part with him when he was a few weeks old so he would not have to grow up despised and taunted as a bastard, but that harsh name would always have the power to shatter his life and break his heart if she let it. Everything he thought he was would collapse around him and the world would look down its nose at the love child of an unwed girl. Even her father wouldn't be able to stop scandal spreading like wildfire and questions being asked about her child's new identity, so she could not let it happen.

She had been little more than a child herself when she had tumbled so headlong in love with her baby's father that nothing else had mattered, but that would only add to the gossips' delicious outrage. Back then she had thought she was the most grown-up and cynical sixteen-year-old ever until she and Joe had remade the world so that he was all she had cared about. She had adored youthful Joseph Briggs with every fibre of her being and the wondrous things they did together—to hell with the petty rules of the *haut ton* or anyone else.

Now she knew their relationship had taken a new turn after her mother died and Joe had been the only one to offer any real comfort. One moment Melissa had been a much-loved only child, enjoying too much freedom and as many tomboyish adventures as she could pack into her busy days, the next her mother's death had ripped through her life with the shock of a ship driven on sharp rocks. She had been lost and desperate for solace, but her father had been so wrapped up in his own grief he had hardly noticed he still had a daughter so, of course, she had turned to the other significant male in her life.

Joe Briggs had been her best secret from the time she was old enough to keep one. He had been her best friend and companion in mischief behind their parents' backs. She had wondered what either set would have made of a farmer's son and the Duke's daughter tumbling from one adventure into the next when they were supposed to be running around their own fields or safely tucked up in bed. They would have been scandalised and furious; she and Joe had known that even as children and had been so careful to keep their friendship a secret.

She was superior and distant with him if they met when she was out riding with her parents or a groom. In secret they had coaxed ponies out at grass or somehow persuaded the least wild of the hill ponies to accept the bridles they had smuggled out of the stables in exchange for sugar or a wrinkled apple and rode them bareback and astride for as long as that day's adventure could last without being found out.

She could almost feel the warm summer breeze heavy with the scents of heather and honey on her face, or the foggy richness of autumn as she thought of them dashing over the moors as fast as their sturdy mounts would take them, laughing or arguing as they went—the thrill of the forbidden adding more spice to the adventure than if their families had approved of their unlikely friendship.

Melissa had turned to Joe for comfort after her father shut himself in his study when his wife had died and refused to see or speak to her because she was so painfully like his dead wife it had unmanned him. Joe had given her sympathy and as much understanding as such a young man had in him with all the generosity in his great heart. He had even tried to curb her angry attempts to shock her father out of isolation and love her again.

The less it worked, the more reckless and openly defiant of the rules of polite society she had become, she remembered with a rueful smile for that confused girl balanced on the edge of womanhood. She had stolen her father's most prized stallion and galloped through the countryside astride and dressed in breeches with her hair flying out loose behind her like a banner, and of course nobody could catch her on that prime piece of horseflesh and uncertain male temper.

Somehow she had survived it and rid herself of two governesses in quick succession amid shocked reports that she was rude and ungovernable and reckless to a fault. Her rebellion had reached its zenith when she had stormed out of church during the vicar's sermon on the divinely allotted roles of man and woman and the essential wickedness of the latter, before and after Eve got poor, innocent Adam evicted from the Garden of Eden with her witchy wiles.

Furious at the pompous littleness of the man's world view and grief for her clever and compassionate mother, who would have been so angry at that veiled rebuke to the Duke's wild daughter, Melissa had run blindly for the familiar shelter of the wind-blown, weather-torn tangle of woods and caves where she and Joe had played and argued as children. There was no point her running home to a father who had given up caring what she thought or did.

Unwilling to attract even more attention to her, Joe had waited until the service was over and ran after her to try to understand her despair at losing both her parents, even if one was still alive. She had been so angry at the vicar, who had thought he could teach sweet feminine compliance by telling women they were inferior and guilty creatures with no right to a will of their own. As she had alternately sobbed and raged, Joe watched her with manly embarrassment, then had bravely overcome it to hold her awkwardly in his arms and try to hug her better.

That was the moment something powerful and a bit frightening had flared into vivid life between them, one hot summer day when the world had suddenly become such a different place that the true wonder of it made her gasp even now. Both of them had been too young to control the suddenly very adult passion that had burned like a firestorm between them, as if it had always been waiting for them to wake up to who and what they were fated to be to one another. Friendship and familiarity had exploded into love and passion, so that first time when they had made love had been more or less by instinct.

Even when it was over and they had opened their eyes on a world so changed by what they could do together, they had felt right in one another's arms and Melissa had refused to be ashamed of herself or him. Joseph Briggs had been her generous, passionate and youthful lover for such a heartbreakingly short space of time, even if her father had dismissed it as sheer stubborn folly and calf love when he had found out what his daughter had been up to while he wasn't paying attention.

Eleven years on from that heady, wondrous, impossible time Melissa knew her young lover would hold her heart until her dying day. She could never settle for anyone less and all she could ever be was alone without him.

'If anything, *you* were too good for *me*,' she whispered into the unnerving silence as she searched through the first stack of papers on the library table.

If only Joe had not died before they had even an inkling he was going to be a father—they would have found a way to be a family together. He was seventeen when he had fallen from the ridge of a high barn roof that he was trying to patch as the rain threatened to ruin the sacks of stored grain below.

When she heard the terrible news that her love had died instantly from a terrible fall, Melissa only wished she had died with him. For all the hope there was in a world without him she might as well have done, and then she had realised she was carrying his child. Loss felt even more bitter when panic raged through her and Joe wasn't there to coax or joke her out of it and make her believe things would come right in the end.

With so much bright young love to bridge the gaps society thought should yawn between them they would have rewritten those stupid rules somehow. Their child would have been all the proof needed they were right and the rest of the world was wrong. Without Joe she had had to tell her father she was carrying a child and there was no chance to marry the father. The shock of her blunt and nervous announcement had stung him to strike at her with furious words because he could never hit her. She had been too busy with her own grief for her mother and her dear and very dead love at the time to see her father had been half-mad with it.

Without her mother to reason with him, he had raged instead of trying to understand what Melissa had done or why she did it. He had called her a slut and a strumpet and an unnatural daughter and, worst of all, a blot on her mother's memory. Shocked and defiantly protective of her unborn child now he had woken up her maternal instincts, Melissa had said some awful things back and the rift had taken a long time to heal. Even now it could feel prickly between them at times, but at least they had been reconciled before her baby was born.

Except she wasn't to know they would be when her father had roused himself from his stupefying grief to organise her entire life for the next however many months it would take to cunningly hide her disgrace. He had been determined there would be just a small hitch in his daughter's life rather than the great aching hole where her lover and best friend once stood.

She was to stay secretly at the remotest house on the Duke's least important estate and wait for her baby to be born while he set up a fine tale of star-crossed lovers fleeing for the border with him in hot pursuit. That tale said His Grace was only just in time to stop the wedding over the anvil and send the mythical would-be groom back to his fortune hunting with his tail between his legs. Apparently the rakes of the *ton* still speculated who the unlucky one was and how much the Duke had had to pay him to keep silent even in his cups.

In the meantime, her maternal grandparents had departed for the Continent to distract themselves from grief for their only daughter and the polite world thought them very noble to take the unruly and defiant Lady Melissa with them. Quite how they kept up that lie was beyond her even now, but she supposed they had never been the kind to take the usual tourist routes or see the sights other curious British tourists longed for after the Treaty of Amiens had been signed and a brief respite from this endless war with France had begun.

While her family set up that tale Melissa had weeks and months of waiting in a silent old house for her baby to be born, and it had changed her from a girl so in love with her dead lover she yearned to die with him into a mother who knew she must live. That reminded her—in the here and now she was a mother on a mission.

So, she gave the ordered mess of a true scholar's library a stern look. If she only had time she could roam the stacks and get a sense of the man who owned them. No, she didn't want to understand the man who even she knew the wags had christened Limping Lord Lathbury; he was an obstacle in her path and that was all most men were after Joe died. Losing him and parting with their baby had hurt so much that risking her heart and soul for love twice in a lifetime was simply not possible. Even if it was, how could she ever confess the truth to a potential husband? He would turn away from her in disgust and probably denounce her, so she would always have to walk alone.

Forgetting the urgency of her quest again, she wrapped her arms round her narrow waist and remembered how wondrous it had felt to have Joe's baby growing and moving inside her and never to be alone for even a second. It was such an intimate bond it had seemed impossible to break, but now her child had no idea she existed. He could live a happy life, though, and that was all that mattered. That was why she was here, risking privacy and reputation, and would go on doing so until her search bore fruit.

'So get on with it, then,' she scolded herself impatiently.

There was nothing in the first stack of books on the library table, so she moved on to a neat pile of notes and ledgers, hoping for a clue since there wasn't the time to examine the library shelf by shelf. Yet her boy was the reason she was here and she could not forget him while she searched for whichever letter Grandmama kept. Plenty had flown between Melissa and her father and maternal grandparents as she pleaded to keep her child before he was born.

They could pretend she was dead so she would live somewhere obscure as a sailor's widow bringing up his posthumous child. Or her child could be passed off as a dead relative's, orphaned and made the Duke's ward so he could live at Wiston Park with them. She had been sure they could think of a way for her to see her child walk and talk and grow up, right up until he was born. However, she had loved him too much to risk the rumours and gossip if he kept the shocking red hair and those light brown eyes that would always give him away as her child.

She sighed at the memory of her beloved, vividly alive little boy and prayed he was happy and healthy. Her feelings hardly mattered, but she had been as content as she ever could be without him or his father while living with her grandparents in the country. Now Grandmama was dead, Melissa was living with her father while she decided what to do with her life.

After she had given up her beloved boy it had felt as if part of her had been cut away, and she could not simply return home as if nothing had happened. All she could do was exist as painlessly as possible and she flatly refused to make her debut. It would be a betrayal to pretend she was the Duke of Wiston's pampered only child without a care in the world, as if Joe and their baby never existed. It was too big a lie and she was so different from those silly, innocent girls with not much on their minds but catching a husband.

Her father had finally agreed she would stay away until she was old enough not to be a debutante. Then her grandmother had needed help nursing Grandpapa. When he had died she could not leave Grandmama alone. There was more grief to bear and her grandmother's correspondence to deal with and Melissa had written the fair copies of Mrs Granger's manuscripts for the printer and the years stretched out without her really noticing. When her grandmother had died, Melissa realised ten years had passed and she didn't want to join the shiny, sophisticated *haut ton* at all.

She and her father had been estranged only for the months it took him to put the tale of her fake elopement about and fool the outside world. It was long enough for their tempers to cool and for him to come to terms with what had happened to his only child while he had been so lost in grief he had hardly noticed he had one. She had believed him when he said he was sorry for the neglect and his hasty temper when he had found out what she and Joe had done before he died.

At least that had made her understand the terrible hollows grief left in a life. She could never be sorry she had loved Joe in every sense of the word before he died so young it hurt her to add up all the years she had lived without him now. She was almost sure Papa had accepted her decision not to be part of polite society or marry some mythical paragon who would accept her refusal to repent her youthful sins that didn't feel in the least bit sinful even now.

Chapter Two

Devil take it, there was a strange woman sitting at his desk, reading one of his books as if her life depended on it! Adam bit back a savage curse and wondered what he had done to deserve it. All evening he had known which of the debutantes had been warned about his scars in advance and those too shocked by them to hide their revulsion. He was here to snatch a few moments to recover his temper or feel it snap and say something disastrous to the next one who paled and looked sick while he did his best to welcome them to his little sister's ball as if he was just a run-of-the-mill sort of lord.

Maybe he should have stayed and told the next one she was a feeble-minded ninnyhammer. Or he could walk out into the night and pace the streets until they had all gone home. Impossible to desert his little sister on her night of nights, though, so he would sip a very small glass of burgundy in blissful solitude and try to regain his sense of humour. Sooner or later he would have to return to his post, but first he wanted privacy and this dratted female was spoiling it.

He had ordered the library door closed and the room kept dark to discourage stray guests, but she had barged in anyway and made herself at home. She was sitting in *his* chair, behind *his* desk, reading *his* book, and anyone would think she owned the place and not him. Still, she would run back to the ballroom as soon as she looked up and saw him staring back at her. He was almost looking forward to watching her bolt with a flutter of incoherent excuses as if she thought his disfigurements might be catching.

Except he didn't want her to jump so violently that she set light to her fiery curls with the branch of candles she was using to study that book so intently. But if he didn't startle her, how was he going to get his library back? He needed a respite and who the deuce was she anyway? He looked more closely as she was so absorbed in his book she would hardly notice if he rode in here on an elephant. No, he was certain he had never set eyes on her before. He would remember her long after he forgot the usual kind of skittish young lady he met nowadays.

If he had met this one in the old days, when he was considered a fine catch on the marriage mart, she would have stood out like a tiger cub in a litter of tame kittens. If she had come along the receiving line tonight he would certainly have noticed. To distract himself from a very male response to her delicious figure, he frowned over the puzzle of how she got in without an invitation. Surely her rich Titian hair and superbly cut dark rose gown were too distinctive for her to be able to flit about the place without being noticed?

Adam made a mental note to improve security in the morning, but at least that gown had obviously been made for her so it wasn't bought second-hand to disguise a clever felon. It fitted her far too perfectly not to have been moulded on her slender curves by a very skilled modiste. Even he knew it was in the first stare of fashion after being shown fashion plates by his grandmother and little sister whenever they were arguing over what was suitable for a debutante and what definitely was not.

This superb creation fell into the latter category and seemed a brave choice for a woman with such richly red hair. And now he was being a lusty male again. He was old enough and ugly enough to know better, so it was high time he stopped leering at strokeable dark rose silk slicked over her slender but womanly curves as if it loved every one of them…

And that's quite enough of that, Lathbury; you may look like a monster, but there's no need for you to act like one as well.

He glared at the hand that had reached towards her as if it wanted to touch so badly it moved without permission from the rest of him.

The slight movement broke her fierce concentration where his hasty entry had failed to and she raised her head impatiently to glare a challenge at him. He waited for the usual look of horror to dawn, but Madame Housebreaker raised her eyebrows haughtily and looked annoyed by his presence in his own library instead. Had he stepped into a different world where he did not own his house, was no longer scarred and lame and women did not flinch away from the very sight of him? No, he was lumbered with this one, so it was only a matter of time before she realised what she was looking at and ran away.

'Who are you?' she demanded huskily instead of flinching and scurrying away.

'You took the words right out of my mouth,' he replied brusquely. Why didn't she have a shrill and squeaky voice instead of that husky contralto to make him long for her to whisper things a scarred lord and mysterious lady housebreaker could never say to one another?

'Ah, then *you* are Lord Lathbury?' she said severely.

'Am I?' he said, feeling his old delight in the ridiculous waking up and stretching. But he told it to go back to sleep. 'Not a difficult deduction, given my infirmities,' he said with an impatient gesture at his damaged face, 'and you have the advantage of me, madam.'

'Oh, that,' she said as if she hardly thought his marred face worth a second glance. It must be a clever lie unless she was terribly short-sighted and too vain to wear spectacles. He doubted it as she surveyed him like an empress displeased with a shabby courtier. 'I am Melissa Aldercombe,' she admitted stiffly.

Lady Melissa looked as if she was bracing herself for his shock at hearing her identity. He tried to glower and pretend he could hardly wait for her to leave, but he was lying—and even more intrigued. 'Lady Melissa,' he said with his usual awkward bow. 'My ballroom is not to your taste, then?' he added clumsily. Even he knew she shunned them and what a stupid question that was.

'On the contrary, it looks very stylish,' she replied airily.

She must have paused to take in the glare and glitter and din of the *ton* at play on her way past then, and that was reckless of her if she wanted to remain a mystery. 'I am sure my grandmother would be delighted to hear that you think so,' he said, 'but I had best not tell her in case we are forced to marry each other to avert a scandal, since you are alone in here with me and neither of us seems to be going away.'

'I wouldn't marry you anyway,' she said, and he tried not to take it personally.

'Of course you don't want to wed a complete stranger, who would?'

'True,' she said and shot him an even warier look. 'I expect your sister's ball will be the talk of the town by morning,' she added brightly.

Naive of her to think it was so easy to divert him from a mystery, and she certainly wasn't plain or disfigured like him to account for her famous liking for solitude; nor was she as arrogant as she wanted him to believe. There was a vulnerability behind her imperious manner that made it look like armour. So, why *had* she spent so many years avoiding her own kind, then?

Something about her careful indifference to even a
scarred old brute like him said she was no man-hater,
but she also seemed blissfully unaware he was having
to fight his base instincts because he was alone with
her while the polite world danced blithely on outside
this room with no idea that a delicious scandal was
brewing under their very noses. He added a peculiar
lack of self-awareness to the puzzle Lady Melissa already was, and something about her touched him in
ways he really didn't want to be touched.

'What are you doing here, Lady Melissa?' he
asked, abruptly hoping a direct question would shock
her into telling him the truth.

'It must be nigh overwhelming for a girl to be
the centre of so much attention so soon after leaving
the schoolroom,' she said, ploughing on with her at-
tempted diversion as if he hadn't spoken. 'Although
Miss Lathbury must be flattered that her family went
to such trouble over her debut,' she added doggedly.

Had she dreamt of a grand fuss over the Duke
of Wiston's daughter once upon a time, then? Half-
forgotten rumours of a much younger Lady Melissa's
wild and rebellious nature, radical views encouraged
by her eccentric maternal grandmother and even
whispers she was mad were clearly ridiculous. The
plot thickened and it was his duty to take a closer
look at the tricky female to find out if he could read
her better across a table than half a room. He might
as well let her have a closer look at his damaged face
and test her mettle while he was about it.

'If you yearn for polite company, you should enter

my house by the front door, Lady Melissa. We would welcome you with open arms, invited or not, and your presence would make Belle's ball into a sensation,' he said, hoping she couldn't tell he was defending himself from her shock when her branch of candles lit his damaged face in merciless detail.

'I can't abide crowded rooms and aimless chatter,' she said without meeting his eye. A one-eyed man did that to a woman, so he should not be surprised or hurt, but somehow he still was.

With her he foolishly longed to be perfect again, or as perfect as a fallible human being ever was. This Adam Lathbury was about as far from the idle society beau who could look her boldly in the eye and demand her sensual attention as it was possible to be and still live. Nothing was ever going to make him a desirable male creature ever again and he wanted to be desired by her nearly as badly as he wanted his next breath.

'How do you know? You have never tried them,' he said as lightly as he could with his heart beating like a drum as he limped even closer. If she was repulsed by his halting gait and various disfigurements, she didn't look it. Maybe it was her lie that had made her look away from his scarred face and the patch over his bad eye and not his repulsive appearance.

'I used to steal down to watch Mama and Papa entertaining as a child,' she said. 'The noise was outrageous and I knew my mother wasn't strong. I used to wish they would just go away and leave us in peace, but apparently we had a position to maintain.'

It seemed unlikely that resentment of her father's

political ambitions had really made her refuse her place in society or that the Duke would have allowed her to give it up so easily. There was a deeper reason for her shunning society and he really wanted to know what it was now he had met her.

Close to, he saw that she was much too distinctive to be lauded as a conventional beauty, but her debut would have been a dazzling success even so. Her gown showed off a perfect figure, but his hungry eyes lingered longest on the sensuous mouth she did her best to pretend was nothing of the sort. With those fiery locks and her guarded amber gaze added to the mix, she would have to fend off suitors by the cartload if she ever did venture into a fashionable ballroom.

She shot him another regal look, as if he was the one who was trespassing, and he wanted her lush mouth soft and wondering and infinitely sensual under his as urgently as a parched man wanted water. Somehow he managed not to stare at her like a hungry wolf, but met her extraordinary lioness eyes, still fighting the delicious dream of her warm and willing in his arms instead of outraged and stiff as the offended aristocrat she would turn into if he tried it.

'I had to steel myself to do my duty tonight, my lady, and maybe you should do the same,' he told her severely. If he could make her angry enough not to notice he was half aroused and struggling hard not to be all the way there, he might save himself one humiliation tonight.

'We have nothing in common,' she said. 'Except

books,' she added with an airy gesture at the shelves all around them.

Did he believe she was so desperate to see his library she had risked this furtive visit in his absence? Not for a single second. Nor was she waiting for an illicit lover; there had been no furtive rattle at the door handle or a flustered male backing away at the sight of him. So what the devil was she up to? 'Why did you steal into my library behind my back?' he demanded with a nod at the book she was shielding with her hands.

'I am a chip off Grandmama's block; a library like yours is too much of a temptation.'

'We both know that's not a good enough reason to risk your privacy and reputation. You broke into my house tonight and I have every right to demand a proper explanation for an outrageous intrusion. So, why are you really here, Lady Melissa?'

'I am too impatient to wait while letters and permissions and chaperons are lined up in order for me to see your fine collection.'

'No! You timed your visit for the one night you thought I was out of the way. If you came here openly you would have to meet me and engineer time alone in here to do whatever you really came for. My sister's ball was a perfect opportunity for you to get in unseen, if you were prepared to risk being caught red-handed and clearly you were. Stop trying to convince me you are here for a good read, my lady. I am not a flat and time is a-wasting.'

'You *are* a very scholarly gentleman,' she said as if flattery might divert him.

'No, I am a very impatient nobleman waiting for an explanation of this outrage.'

'Maybe I am too shy to come in daylight,' she said sulkily.

'And maybe not.'

'I prefer books to people, my lord, and luckily for both of us it's not a crime.'

How could he persuade her to confide in him when she was so determined not to? Something told him she needed help. Whatever secret made her brave the uproar and scandal if she was found here by anyone but Limping Lord Lathbury he had no idea, but there were so many layers of armour around her it might need gunpowder to get past it. He saw her hand shake when she pushed a stray curl of her vivid hair behind her ear in a gesture that betrayed her agitation, and he felt his heartbeat jar with pity and something a lot more worrying.

Lady Melissa was doing her best to hide her true self behind a bland front, but he felt as if something momentous had happened when he found her in here. When he opened the door he would have given half his fortune to avoid company, but hers was intriguing and forbidden and she should have been a lot more careful when she stepped inside his lair.

He could be deluding himself about the instant feeling of a sensual connection flaring to life between them at first sight being mutual. Maybe he was just a fool who had not bedded a woman for so long he ached like a lecherous youth for her, and wouldn't it be wonderful if he wasn't hideous and she wanted him back?

If he were still the man he had once been, perhaps she would yearn for him right back. In the heady peace and inviting shadows of this suddenly intimate room, all the things they could do to one another— if only wishes were horses so beggars could ride— ran through his mind like refined torture. It was one fantasy too many for a man trying to get his base instincts under control. He had just faced a ballroom full of the loveliest and brightest beauties high society boasted and failed to want a single one of them, so what was so special about her? Apart from a superb figure, glorious red hair, piquant features and those lush pink lips parted as if asking him a question he was longing to answer with heat and need and a large helping of desperation.

Chapter Three

Any other lord would have already ordered her out of his private sanctum. He might have given his word not to admit she had been here since he wanted to avoid a sensational distraction from the business of launching Miss Lathbury on to the marriage mart. Of course any ordinary sort of lord would probably not have come in here in the first place. Melissa sensed this one was very near to the end of his tether when he had entered the room and, after all the stares and whispers he must have endured, she supposed it was hardly to be wondered at.

It felt novel and a little dangerous to be alone with such a powerful man and so deep inside his lair. She already felt as if she knew more about him than he wanted her to, and he was certainly not the wreck her cousin Phillida's letters described after the terrible accident that had left him scarred and limping.

Her cousin had mourned his ruined looks and fine physique, but this man was deeper than such a favourite of the gods. Melissa doubted such a fine young man would ever become so intriguing and out of the common way as this mature, much-tried one in front of her now was, from the tip of his sternly controlled dark curls to his lordly toes.

Perhaps it was as well if he thought he was a monster so he had no idea about this silly fizz of attraction sharpening her senses and fogging her brain when she badly needed it to be sharp and invent a way to get her out of here without a scandal. She hadn't felt such sharp and deep-down heat flower inside her since Joseph was alive, and Lord Lathbury was a complete stranger, for goodness' sake.

She resented the reawakening of all this fire and sensuality she had considered Joe's alone until she met him. Now she wanted unthinkable things from a man she had met minutes ago. Whatever was she thinking of? The answer was she wasn't thinking at all, just looking and wanting, and that would never do.

A shiver chilled her spine at the thought of him reading the letter she was here to find and it brought her back to earth with a sickening thump. He would condemn the girl she had once been for loving so fiercely that none of the rules had mattered.

Even if he didn't broadcast her sins to the world, his good eye would blast her with his contempt and that sensual, sensitive mouth of his would harden to a disapproving line. Then something young and wild and promising inside her would have to die all over again. No, it wouldn't. It was already dead—and buried in her lover's grave. All she had left was their son and she would do anything to protect him.

Reminded of why she was here, she managed to eye him warily instead of hungrily. Surely he would have to return to his guests soon? If she persuaded him not to give her away, she could slip back into the night and find another way to search his collection. Maybe she should have let her father approach him openly and appeal for the return of her property. Maybe she could trust this man's integrity far enough not to read through it and find out what was so important about it. However, maybes were never going to be good enough when her son's happiness was at stake.

'I never gossip,' he said gently, as if he had given up ordering her to tell him why she was here and was trying to coax it out of her instead.

He shifted his weight from one leg to the other as if he were stiff after standing for so long being stared at this evening, and she tried not to feel even more drawn to him than she was already. How he must have hated playing host tonight, but he'd done it for his little sister. Maybe it had taken his bravery to make her see she had taken the easiest route available to her by living with her grandparents for all those years, but this wasn't about her. She must concentrate on why she was here instead of his fascinating quirks and vulnerabilities.

'You have avoided society for so many years yet you risked coming here tonight. What is so crucial you stole in here behind my back on a night when any fool might have found you here?' he persisted, and panic raced through her like fast poison.

Had he already read her letter? Was he playing with her before he told the wide world what she'd done? Even if he was, she couldn't dart round him and dash out into the night. But if he knew he would be eyeing her with contempt instead of curiosity, wouldn't he?

She took a deep breath and unclenched her hands. Papa was right; she *had* spent too many years away from the world for her own good. She tried to read Lord Lathbury's thoughts in the wary dark eye he seemed to see a great deal better with than most people did with two, but he was far too good at hiding them. Another shiver cut through her despite the fires burning at both ends of this room.

'Why do you shun society when your looks and birth should set you at the pinnacle of it, Lady Melissa?' he added like a duellist slipping a cleverly disguised feint into his opponent before they realised how dangerous he was.

'Why do you?' she countered warily.

'Tit for tat,' he explained blandly, 'I avoid society to save it the trouble of avoiding me.'

Exactly, the Melissa who longed to be straightforward wanted to agree. 'They could be pining for your company,' she suggested instead.

'I think we both know they prefer my room to my company,' he said stiffly—as if he thought she was baiting him.

'Really?' she said unwarily, shocked if other women

could not or would not see past his physical scars to the strong and vibrant man in his prime underneath them. Did they really not want him as a lover when she could easily make a fool of herself if he desired her as much as she did him? Oh, no! That was it, of course it was—she wanted him, like a lover, like a magnet wanted iron.

The wild, heedless Melissa of all those years ago was trying to take charge of her thoughts and actions now and she had so wanted to believe the wench was dead. Maybe she had been until tonight and drat the man for resurrecting the needy little minx who had caused such chaos for herself and her family last time.

'Yes. Would you like to come outside and greet me in front of my guests so you can give them the lie, then?' he said as if he thought she really was mocking him so he might as well retaliate.

That wild girl whispered, *Accept his dare and slap it right back at him. Let him stand with you and defy the world if he really wants this out in the open.*

Luckily, rational Melissa was never going to let that happen. 'I dislike loud noise and abhor gossip,' she said instead.

'Weak,' he said as if he could read the conflict under her stiff words.

'And now you are being rude, my lord,' she told him crossly. He raised his eyebrows at her sitting here in his chair and in his library as if she was the one who owned them. She blushed, and wasn't it hard enough having carroty hair without this tendency to flush like a peony?

'The gossips hated my mother for marrying a duke when she was only gently born,' she added as if that might explain everything and even she knew it didn't, but maybe if she wished hard enough he would accept her limp excuse and leave her alone in here.

'I doubt she cared. If you tell me why you are here, I might be enough of a gentleman to go away,' he said, and clearly she was wishing for the moon.

'I came to look for something that can only have value for me,' she said cautiously, and peace of mind was priceless so it wasn't even a lie.

'Hmm,' he said with a sharp look at her hands folded protectively over the book in front of her.

She unclasped them and tried to look unconcerned.

'The auction catalogue from my most recent purchases?' he said, and drat the man for reading it upside down. 'Not something the usual kind of housebreaker would risk jail for.'

Tension seemed to lock every sinew in her body so painfully tight it felt as if she might break if he leaned over and took it from her.

'Ah, yes, of course—The Granger Collection,' he said after scanning the page she was trying so hard to memorise when he had entered and she had forgotten to watch out for stray lords. 'And Mrs Granger was your maternal grandmother.'

'Yes,' she admitted wearily. 'My cousin sold off our grandmother's collection although she left it to me. He would forbid women any education except sewing and learning to order a fine menu if he could.'

'So you are trying to track down her books?'

'Indeed,' she said warily, and at least it wasn't a lie, she did want them back and they were rightfully hers.

'Then why didn't you write to me and ask for them back? I would not keep a single book that rightfully belonged to someone else.'

'Then you are a very unusual book collector indeed, Lord Lathbury.'

'You have a point; a rare volume is like catnip to bookworms,' he said with a smile that made her heart leap, then race. 'I have known one swear he never even set eyes on a book he had begged to borrow so he didn't have to give it back, but I am an honourable man.'

'You might share my cousin's poor opinion of female scholars so how was I to know you would not dismiss a letter asking for them back?'

'But his actions were illegal.'

'As he was cunning enough to sell my grandmother's books and papers before I found out and tried to stop the sale, I suspect possession is nine-tenths of the law. Some of the books can be replaced, but they would not be the ones she owned then. There are notes scribbled in them in her hand,' she managed to say coolly enough.

'Then tell the auction house they must have everything that was sold without your permission returned immediately.'

'Oh, yes, and I'm sure that will work,' she said scathingly. It didn't matter; she had lost his full attention and felt stupidly piqued by his distracted air instead of glad his thoughts were busy elsewhere.

* * *

Adam listened to a change in the far-off sounds of music and frowned. The relentless beat of the dance was winding to a halt. There was a pause, then a more aimless tune played and that must have been the supper dance. 'I must go,' he said and saw eagerness in her intriguing eyes this time. 'You can tell me all about it later, Scheherazade.'

'No, I must go.'

'Unless you walk through that door with me and announce your presence to the world you can forget leaving here just yet.'

'You can't make me stay. I got in here without being seen and can leave whenever I like.'

'I intend to ensure nobody ever does that again; you could have been anyone,' he said and nearly laughed out loud at her outraged look. She glared at him like a warrior princess ready to order him locked in a dungeon until he learned some manners. 'Give me your word to be here when I return, so I don't have to set someone to guard the door and stop you from leaving my lair behind my back.'

'You wouldn't do that; you don't want to be the butt of scandal any more than I do.'

'*I* have nothing to hide,' he told her with a lazy smile.

'You will if we are found alone together.'

'Don't tempt me. My grandmother is always telling me how badly I need a wife and there's not exactly a queue of willing young ladies eager to take me on.'

'You can't want to marry me.'

'I suspect the boot is on the other foot, but never mind it now, time's a-wasting,' he pointed out with an airy gesture towards his ballroom.

'Indeed,' she said with a smug look in the same direction to say she thought she held the best cards.

'I suppose a shop-soiled baron will be a comedown for the daughter of a duke, but needs must when the devil drives,' he said and sat down in the nearest armchair to take his ease like the careless Bond Street beau he used to be.

'I'm not the marrying kind,' she said curtly.

'You will be when someone comes looking for me. They must be wondering where I am by now.'

'Go and do your duty then, unless you want your sister's ball gossiped about for all the wrong reasons.'

'Belle is even more eager to marry me off than my grandmother,' he said, 'and as you are quite an elderly spinster maybe you could do worse.' He managed not to laugh as she shot more fury at him. The light from those candles lovingly picked up vibrant lights in her truly red curls doing their best to escape a battalion of hairpins. She was magnificent and he was having far too much fun teasing her—of course she didn't want to marry him, what female in her right mind would?

'I wouldn't marry you if the Queen walked in on us,' she said, confirming that conclusion, and what else did he expect?

He tried to stamp on the idea that it would be so intriguing to marry a mystery woman and unwrap all her secrets layer by fascinating layer that he would never have time to be bored or self-conscious or sensitive about his many and varied flaws. He could be the one man who was going to know Melissa Aldercombe to the core as they battled and loved together for life. And here was Bad Adam again, slavering like a hungry wolf at the very thought of finding the true heart of her and plunging right in with greedy sensuality.

Maybe it was good to know there was some life left in him under Limping Lord Lathbury's dour exterior after all, perhaps, but he was no prize for even the most desperate spinster lady to net herself. Dorinda had taught him how little value he had as a suitor after the accident ruined his looks. At least the very thought of his former fiancée sobered him. Bad Adam would have to howl for the moon and live with this gnawing need for the unique and delicious Lady Melissa Aldercombe.

Memory of how it felt to be flatly rejected by a woman he had thought loved him as much as he had loved her stung him back to the reality of who he was now, and how the hell any woman would ever truly want him again was beyond him. But he was probably right about how much love they had truly felt for one another, shallow Lord Lathbury and lovely Dorinda Merriot, the toast of St James's. The happy accord of two selfish and fine young creatures faded like mist in the sun when he changed from Adonis to Cyclops that day. Who could blame lovely, charming and accomplished Dorinda for taking one look at the wreck he had become and ending the engagement? Certainly not him, but at the time it had felt like the final blow that must break him.

Now he was so relieved they were not already wed when he was maimed because Dorinda's reaction to his spoiled face had said she would never share a room with him again without flinching, let alone the marriage bed. The idea of being endured by his wife made him feel sick and reminded him to keep his stupid passions to himself as well.

'Luckily for me I am not easily hurt,' he lied. He still had to find out what Lady Melissa was really up to, though, or goodness knew whose library she would creep into next, and some of his fellow bibliophiles were dreadful old roués under their dusty disguises.

'I still won't marry you,' she told him.

She had no idea how much he liked the idea of such an extraordinary Lady Lathbury sharing his everything, but it was unthinkable. He was a reckless idiot who had crashed his phaeton and killed his best friend. The past sucked him into the darkest time in his life, and of course he couldn't tie her to such a monster. He was repulsive to look at and a blockhead. He had set off in the dark, almost too drunk to stay in the driving seat of his racing curricle, for a bet. His tiger had wisely refused to go with him, so his best friend, Lord Rufus Frensham, had volunteered to help Adam win the ridiculous wager he would reach Brighton before sun up.

Adam had driven his high-spirited four-in-hand so fast they were a few miles from Brighton just as the sun was about to come over the horizon. The first glimmers of it had almost blinded his stinging eyes and raked his aching head with a breath of common sense at exactly the wrong moment, and he barely had time to rise in his seat in order to have enough power to pull hard on the reins to shift his team just far enough away from the petrified child spreadeagled in the road not to run him over. The boy had stumbled as he ran from the wild-eyed foaming team and they had been going too fast to stop.

Adam had just one frozen moment to watch the fine old oak tree on the other side of a shallow ditch they were about to drive into rushing ever closer and hear his terrified horses scream with fear. He would always remember the grim set of Ru's pale face as Death rushed towards him with scythe raised just before impact and black oblivion sucked him into a merciful darkness.

Adam had woken all too soon to agony everywhere in his broken body. He had been thrown so hard on to the hedge it had torn his face and broken his limbs, but the worst torture of all had been seeing Ru laid out, still and unmistakably dead, where the grim-faced rescuers had left him as beyond human help. Adam had heard the shots as some kind soul put an end to two of his precious greys' suffering and he had remembered begging them to shoot him, too, as they lifted him off that damned hedge a fraction of an inch at a time. Even five years on the thought of it made him squirm.

Rather than face what he had done, he had asked good men to put him out of his misery, like the horses he had damaged so wilfully and so terribly the front pair had no chance of surviving their injuries and even the rear pair had never been the same again. He had deserved the looks of horror from those brave men when he was not sure he could have faced the ordeal he had put them through even today. Their eyes had slid away from the sight of him and, by heaven, he must have been a spectacle fit to terrify an army surgeon.

Afterwards Dorinda's rejection of him had felt like a just punishment for his folly. Later it was more of a blessed release, but at the time he had thought his heart was broken along with his body. So, no, he didn't deserve to wed a red-haired enchantress if they were caught here, and she certainly didn't deserve to end up saddled with a broken-down fool.

It still felt impossible to let her walk out of here with that sale catalogue, though, knowing she was intent on her next hare-brained scheme to find what she was looking for. It must mean a great deal to make the risk of coming here worthwhile, but whatever it was, she must stay here while he got hosting supper out of the way because he couldn't endure the thought of her wandering home alone in the pitch-dark to her father's grand mansion in the next square over.

'If you are not found here, there will *be* no scandal and you won't need to refuse me publicly and privately,' he told her as if he almost thought it was a joke as well.

'I wouldn't marry you anyway.'

'Of course you wouldn't, I'm a monster,' he admitted gruffly.

'Oh, stop being so sorry for yourself. It's even more maddening than when you're acting so arrogantly I could cheerfully smack you,' she told him with an infuriated shake of her head. Another curl escaped captivity and all the rampant fantasies he should not be having, of all of them lying loose on her naked shoulders as she gazed at him with heat and adoration in her amber gaze, instead of all that ice and offended dignity, thundered back into rampant life and made him move deeper into the shadows so she couldn't see how aroused he was.

'Give me your word you won't leave before I finish playing host again,' he said tersely.

'No, go away.'

'I don't want to,' he said, and it was all too true. What he wanted was to kiss her breathless and seduce her secrets out of her one by one. Although that was impossible, he still had to find out what she was up to and stop her plunging headlong into even more trouble as soon as his back was turned.

'If it's the only way to get you to go away, I will promise,' she said resentfully.

'What are you promising?'

'To stay here and wait, since I can think of nothing worse than having to wed you for propriety's sake,' she said with furious clarity.

'There wouldn't be much propriety involved after I got you to the altar, my lady,' he warned her shortly and limped away while she was still staring at him as if she couldn't quite believe her ears.

Slipping the key from inside to outside as he passed

through, he locked the door behind him. 'Strategy, my lady,' he whispered and tucked the key into his waistcoat pocket. Now all he had to do was forget he had fascinating and furious Melissa Aldercombe locked in his library and calm his rabid fantasies of her as hot and ready for him as he was for her the instant he had met her eyes across his shadowy book room. He wasn't sure there was that much forgetting in the world, but he had been raised a gentleman and sunk to being a monster, so it should be easier than this to remember she could never truly want a breakdown like him.

He braced himself for his grandmother's silent reproach for his tardiness and more sidelong glances at his marred face from his guests. He even managed to blandly return the first of them with a raised eyebrow as he slipped into the room. He tried hard to look as if he had been recruiting his strength all this time in blessed solitude, instead of longing to be Lady Melissa's latest and most unlikely secret of all.

Chapter Four

Melissa could hardly believe the wretch had locked her in. She felt like a half-tamed beast he thought would cause havoc if he left her free and it made her furious that he was probably right. She would have broken her promise if he had given her the choice to stay here and keep her word. She jiggled the door knob impatiently and of course it didn't move. Now he was out there, pretending to be a polite and chastened lord, the duplicitous, arrogant devil.

She turned away from the door with an expletive her father would be shocked to know she had even heard of, let alone used. How annoying that she had never learnt to pick locks so she could not confound him with an empty room when he came back. She was trapped in here until His lordly Lordship chose to let her out again.

For a while she wasted her energy thinking up suitable punishments for him, like boiling in oil or being forced to dance with a whole parade of debutantes. That would be the worst punishment of all as those silly girls tried to dance with a man they refused to look at full on. She shook her head at their folly and his low opinion of his masculine charms. He was a mature and compelling man with vital presence and sharp intelligence. Then there was his gruff humour—perhaps that explained this odd feeling she had known him far longer than mere minutes.

When she had first looked up and seen him staring back at her it felt as if she had known him already and that was such a strange idea she didn't even want to think about it. Then there was a wicked stir of excitement deep inside her she had all but forgotten. Apparently another man *was* capable of stirring her inner wanton to fiery and instant life with one look. That would teach her to be smug about the smooth course her life was sure to take once she found that letter and made up her mind what to do with the rest of it.

She had had to fight past her fascination with the man to recall where they were and what she was doing here all the time they were talking. She knew the dashing Lord Lathbury and Lord Rufus Frensham had once set out for Brighton after a heavy night of drinking that ended in tragedy. She had heard how they had spent the evening drinking and gambling in the sort of low dive where dashing and reckless gentlemen with too much time and money went when they were bored with their privileged lives.

Drunken idiots, she had thought dismissively when she read about it in her cousin Phillida's letters. At the time she had thought Phillida was a little in love with the man and reported the end of his engagement with unseemly glee, but if the lovely Miss Merriot had fitted the charming rake he once was, how would she have coped with this deeper, darker version of Lord Lathbury if she had been brave enough to marry him anyway? It felt wrong to be glad the lady hadn't been brave enough to risk it.

How would Lady Melissa Aldercombe have felt if she had wanted another woman's husband as much as she was trying not to want Lord Lathbury at this very moment? Whatever he was back then, he looked like a schoolgirl's wildest fantasy of a dashing pirate lover now, but she wasn't one of those and she didn't want her head turned, especially not by a man who wouldn't want her served naked on a silver platter if he knew the truth about her. Heaven forbid that he ever did!

Despite the harsh reality of the thought of him being horrified by what she had done for love at sixteen, she couldn't help a smile when she thought of him out there in his own ballroom right now. No doubt he was being gruff and guarded with any of the guests who had come here tonight to gawp at him and not admire his sister. He had such a skewed idea of how he looked, but that was no excuse for locking her in here, and the idea of him kissing her and bringing her wild inner Melissa fully back to wild and glorious life again was totally impossible.

So, where was she with real life, then? Ah, yes, she must use his absence to write the names of the other buyers from his sale catalogue out to get a head start on finding the other books while she thought out a plan to get back in here and search his in peace. If he stayed away long enough, she could look for them and maybe even make a start on scanning through them for her letter.

Adam felt he had been battered all over with a soft mallet by the time he escaped the most persistent of the society matrons. Apparently matchmaking mamas had not written him off as a potential husband for one of their darlings after all.

More fool you for thinking being maimed would get you off the hook, Lathbury, he told himself disgustedly.

They should ask their charges before they hatched plans to marry them to the highest bidder, though. As a debutante dodged behind her dance partner to avoid him, he imagined the girl's horror if he had stopped to ask her to dance with him instead. He didn't want to be tolerated for his money and title.

At least Lady Melissa had taken no notice of his infirmities after a sceptical look as if to say *What on earth is the fuss about?* But she was a rare female and made the cream of the *ton* seem as dull as ditchwater as he waited for an excuse to slip back to his library and feel fully alive again, something he had failed to feel during five long years of trying to be a better man than the idiot who had killed his best friend.

Adam whiled away a few more minutes pretending to be quite happy he was part of this circus for his sister's sake. He wondered what Lady Melissa would think of it close up. To him it seemed noisy, overheated and tedious. He could hardly believe he had once revelled in overcrowded rooms and all this deafening social chatter. He evaded another ambitious mama with a lukewarm smile and a gesture at the card room to say he was very busy playing host so he could not discuss her charge's sweet nature and many ladylike accomplishments right now.

In the card room itself intense-looking games of whist and piquet were going on, along with a slightly more frivolous one of silver loo. Nobody was taking much notice of him so he slipped out of the other door to check the supper room as if he was intent on his duties and not a rapid escape. Luckily it was empty except for a few ravaged plates and abandoned glasses, so it was easy to stroll in and out the other side without anyone taking much notice.

The service corridor was deserted, so he strolled towards the library and wilfully neglected his duty for the second time tonight. He slid the key into the lock and was inside the room with the door locked behind him before Lady Melissa could do whatever she planned to do in order to escape his villainous clutches.

'I hope you're proud of yourself,' she said instead of trying to hit him with the nearest heavy object as he half expected her to. 'You locked me in here like a beast in a cage, so I shall always know to expect the worst of you from now on.'

Yes, expect that and double it, his inner demons prompted as he bit back a groan of sensual awareness.

She was so certain she had herself under tight control, so unaware how delicious she looked as she glared at him from his chair, which would never be the same for him again either. He would never be able to sit there and think through complex and challenging concepts clearly, because he would be thinking of this complex and challenging woman sitting in it now instead and dreaming of what might have been if he wasn't a monster and she wasn't an aristocratic single lady.

'Good, so I can misbehave and you won't bat an eyelid,' he tried to tease her and lighten the mood, because the very idea of sitting in his chair with her warm and willing in his arms made him feel downright dangerous.

'You know perfectly well that's not what I meant,' she told him with a frown that woke up even more of his inner devils.

Confound it, why couldn't he want one of the eligible young ladies out in his ballroom instead of mysterious Lady Melissa? She was the remote, aloof, unknowable Lady Melissa Aldercombe. The Duke of Wiston's only child, and she was above his touch even if he wasn't hideous. There, that was one or two devils slain and if he kept on doing it she might still get out of here unmolested.

'Then you should not say it, should you?' he said so coolly she ought to be offended, and that would be good, wouldn't it? Except she looked even more delicious with her feathers ruffled and temper in her extraordinary eyes as he limped closer and had to fight this devilish awareness of her as a woman at every step.

'You are the most infuriating man I have ever met, Lord Lathbury,' she told him. Was that a flush on her high cheekbones and a glint of something else in her eyes, or was he guilty of wishful thinking?

Probably, he told himself and clamped down on desire even harder because if he didn't she would notice, and he didn't want those amber eyes of hers turning cold and contemptuous again. 'Since you don't appear to have met many I am hardly top of a long list.'

'I hope I never meet one more arrogant than you since I couldn't keep a civil tongue in my head.'

'It's hardly civil to call me so when you know a gentleman can't reply in kind.'

'You haven't proved to be much of one so far,' she grumbled, and he had a terrible urge to lean over and kiss her sulky mouth to demonstrate how very wrong she was.

'You had better not try me too hard then, had you, Lady Melissa?' he warned her softly.

'What? You mean…' Her words trailed off as if she could hardly believe her ears.

Now she was looking at him as if the idea had woken a feminine curiosity that made it nigh impossible for him to resist the need to watch her go wild with sensual delight in his arms. There was so much passion locked up in her lioness's gaze, such rich promise he dared not think about right now. They had only just met and he was damaged and embittered. But she still looked wide-eyed with the shock of knowing he wanted her, and her mouth was half-open in a delicious pout of surprise.

Then her eyelids went heavy and her pout turned to a luscious, secretive smile before she let her mind catch up. She pursed them sternly as if she was trying to convince them both she had no idea what he meant and her gaze slid away from his. She shook her head as if convincing herself he couldn't possibly mean what she thought he did. She was such a puzzling mix of sensuality and innocence he went from lustful to protective and back again as contrary emotions chased across her face as well.

'I am still a man, Lady Melissa, for all I look like a mere shadow of one,' he said huskily and heard the frustration in his own voice and hoped she didn't notice it.

'You look like the ordinary, aggravating sort to me, Lord Lathbury,' she argued with a glare to say he should stop dwelling on his infirmities.

'You have no idea how dangerous a man can be if you think the worst I can do to you is look,' he warned her rather desperately. He clenched a fist behind his back to keep it busy while she stared back at him as if he was no threat. By the heavens, he should be!

'Pah, I dare say I can run faster than you,' she said recklessly.

'You were saying?' he asked her, trying to pretend he was breathless from moving so fast. She was out of his chair and in his arms before she could even think about dodging away. He was only warning her how vulnerable she was to marauding males. He just wanted to stop her provoking the one who had her locked in his library for future reference.

'In a fair race,' she argued just as breathlessly, and she didn't have to stretch every nerve and sinew to get here. Now he had her in his arms her eyes widened in shock, but she still didn't say the *No* he needed to hear. He waited for it as she watched him with heavy-lidded eyes and lips parted as if she could taste the sweet promises of intimacy like good baking.

He watched her lick her lips and knew he had been right all along: the delicious softness of finest silk over warm, womanly curves was sensual and shattered his good resolutions that he would warn her what she was inviting by coming into a man's library alone then let her go. He felt her gasp and sigh instead of just hearing it, and heat thundered through him. Temptation screamed as his touch on the strokcable stuff under his hands became firmer and she felt as on fire as he was, but how could she be? He was still a beast and she was still lovely and so desirable he had lost the words that were supposed to warn her what she was risking if she was too innocent to feel it for herself.

This wasn't going according to his plan. He had thought he could teach her how vulnerable she was to predatory males by grabbing her like one and showing her his strength was more than hers, so she would never risk another bookworm's library, never mind what her secrets were. The thunder of her heartbeat as he curved her even more intimately against his body made him simply want her—and never mind lessons in resisting rakes.

She didn't *feel* scared—she felt delicious and right against his eager body. He met her eyes and saw dreamy curiosity in the gold and amber depths. If this was the real Lady Melissa, he wanted her with everything he once was and longed to be again. But he was a limping and unsightly beast. She must be searching for the right words to condemn him as a randy animal, and he tried to persuade himself he must let her go with a suitably ashamed apology.

It was so long since she felt it that Melissa had almost forgotten how loud and insistent the roar of mutual desire was, and now it was in full cry. Last time it demanded like this she was a giddy young girl. Until tonight she had been so convinced she was immune to ever hearing it again that she had forgotten to guard against it and found out she had been lying to herself all these years. All it took was the wrong man to stir her inner hedonist into a heady mix of curiosity and desperation.

Adam Lathbury had woken up a fire even hotter and wilder than that which she had felt when she was almost too young to know what it was. She fought to remember all the reasons she should hate him, yet he was so close and it had been so long since she was close to another human being like this and wanting everything from him. Something about him called to her as no man had since she was head over heels in love with Joe.

She took a hungry breath of air and caught in the scent and warmth and heat of this strong and damaged man with it and that only made things worse. She wanted to breathe him in and learn far too much about him, then wrap him into her deepest sensual memory for ever, but she would enjoy the illusion of something wonderful before he remembered who they were and let her go.

'Kiss me?' she muttered huskily.

'Gladly,' he whispered, and then it was too late to change her mind.

He kissed her as if he had been starving for too long and like the best dream she had ever had. Yes, that was what it was—it was a delicious dream. She had fallen asleep waiting for him to come back and let her go. Now she was fantasising about being so deliciously close to the man she had first glimpsed standing on the edge of his own ballroom earlier tonight as if he thought he didn't belong there. He had seemed isolated and apart from the gaiety and intrigue going on around him, an outsider looking in.

She had felt the connection of one lonely soul to another then, even as she told herself not to be ridiculous and get on with why she was here in the first place. So it might be fate if they really were kissing one another now, if it wasn't a dream. As it was one of those, she might as well step right into it and lose herself in the fantasy.

In her wickedly inventive dream he smoothed a sensuous touch down her backbone and moulded her even tighter against him, body to sweetly aching

body; mouth on hungry mouth. The feel of his torso
hard with all the extra muscle he must have devel-
oped to compensate for his injuries destroyed any last
caution hiding in a dark corner arguing this was real.

Dream Melissa let her hands roam and stretched
on tiptoe to test the hard strength of him against her
slighter, softer and sleeker body. She was greedy to
see and feel and know everything about him, never
mind his old wounds or her more hidden ones. He
was power and heat, gentleness and supplication, and
what a contrary man he was, she decided with a tender smile against his teasing mouth.

Then his kiss deepened and begged for more. He
sent hot, sweet heat shooting through her with his
wicked tongue until she whimpered with need and
opened for him and demanded right back. Oh, yes,
that was it; more, she wanted more and she wanted
him, so very much. She let him know it by tangling
her tongue with his and still managed a hungry moan,
as if to say *Better, my lord, but still not enough.*

She felt wild heat tempting and taunting and molten
as she reached her hands around his neck to get even
closer to him. She wanted to meld his feasting, wondrous mouth even closer to hers. Now his clever fingers
caressed the fine skin along her jaw and up to tease the
shivering sensitivity under her ear and smooth back
again to where heat still sparked and tingled.

It felt as if her legs had turned to water with such
intense pleasure and she wobbled even closer to his
mighty body for support. She felt his hands shake
and mutual want and hunger and whatever this was

melted another layer of isolation between them. It only made her want him even more.

Silly man, she chided him silently and cupped her hand over his exploring one, held it against her face for a moment to try to say without words that nobody else but he could do this to her or for her. Heat burned wild inside her because it was Adam, not because this was her first passionate kiss for over a decade.

She groaned a protest when he broke their long, hot kiss to replace his fingers with his mouth and trail kisses along her neck where they had been creating havoc. It felt so good she bowed back to give him un-fettered access to her vulnerable throat and felt him flinch at the extra strain she put on his damaged body.

'Oh, no, I'm sorry,' she gasped, jumping back from them with her hand over her kiss-shocked mouth to keep in all the things she wanted to say and knew he would hate to hear. Because, of course, this was real and she had just behaved shamelessly in his arms!

And she loathed the idea of hurting him physically or mentally. She could tell from his pained dark gaze he thought she had recoiled because she found him less of a man than she wanted him to be, and noth-ing could be further from the truth.

'I hurt you,' she explained numbly. Somehow she had to convince him it wasn't the sudden realisation she was kissing him and not some perfect, pleased-with-himself society rake that made her step back from them.

Chapter Five

'Ah, don't, Melissa. Don't dare apologise to me,'
Lord Lathbury said shakily, looking as if it was truly
the last thing he wanted.

She had better try harder to be sorry that their
closeness ended so suddenly, then. Wild heat still
shook and shocked through her as she forced air into
her lungs and stepped back from him on clumsy-
feeling legs to stare up at him with who knew what
in her eyes. She was still shivering with need and,
yes, she *was* ashamed of herself. He must think every
harsh rumour he had ever heard about her wildness
and ungovernable nature was true after such a perfect demonstration that the Duke of Wiston's daughter was every bit as feral as the gossips said she was.

Melissa almost believed it herself when she com-
pared how she should be with how she was with him.
No, she reminded herself sternly, she had done what
she did with Joe because he was the love of her life.
She would not let the gossip and speculation taint her

dear, lost love even if it meant turning away from this very different man and strangling this misbegotten need for every passion man and woman could share considering what that had led to last time.

'Are you all right?' she could not stop herself asking him even so. She saw him flinch as if the question hurt him far more than any extra strain they had put on his damaged body. He stepped further away from her as if they had stung one another, not summoned sensual magic together.

'How can you even ask me that, Melissa? I forced myself on you like a hardened rake.'

'Hardly,' she argued huskily. 'I know you would have let me go if I managed to work up as much as a whimper of protest.'

'My inner gentleman wasn't in charge at the time,' he warned her bleakly.

Silence and a crackle from the fire sounded like a gunshot even with the music from the ballroom still faintly audible. The world was rattling on as they tried to pretend nothing much had happened here. Her heart ached and after that fiery kiss it felt like a betrayal to rebuild her barriers again and leave him on the outside. She wanted to hug herself to keep the ache and the wonder inside, but it would give away the pleasure and the pain of denying it away again. So she was right; it was only ever a dream. This scarred and honourable man and Lady Melissa Aldercombe could never be more than one of those to each other.

'You'd better have this,' he said, fumbling in the pocket of his dark evening coat.

His clumsiness said he was as shaken by that passionate kiss and its unsatisfactory ending as she was, but he held out the key of the door and silently invited her to take it all the same. She raised her hand and he dropped it on to her palm as if he dare not touch her, so maybe that kiss was extraordinary for him as well, even if it looked as if it was never, ever going to be repeated from the stern look in his undamaged eye.

'Why?' she asked, and it felt hard to shape the words with a mouth that remembered his on it so fondly. The loss of it felt painful, but she shook her head at her own stupidity and backed even further away from him.

'I should have thought it was obvious,' he said huskily.

'No.'

'Try for some sense, Lady Melissa,' he said as if her refusal to pretend they had been discussing the weather was rasping him raw. 'And promise you will never give a man so much control over your body and your freedom again.'

'No, I have feelings and needs like the next person; you can't stop me having them.'

'I can try,' he said with a heavy sigh.

She didn't want to be a sore conscience or a duty to him. 'Please don't,' she said with a bitter sigh of her own.

'What if I had refused to stop? If we had gone much further, even I am not sure I could have done and you don't seem to realise how rash and idiotic it was to come here alone and unprotected even now.'

'I am an adult with a mind and temper of my own,' she said with a glance towards her cloak and the pistol lying on top of it to say she was quite capable of protecting herself, thank you very much.

'And how would you feel if you had to wound or kill a man with that toy, even if you did remember to keep it within reach? Taking a life is a heavy burden to bear.'

His raw agony said how bitterly he regretted his friend's death and she wanted to shout at him that not everything that happened that day could have been his fault. Yes, he was a drunken fool to set out on a reckless midnight drive for a stupid wager. No doubt he was driving too fast with journey's end in sight, but he didn't put a child in the path of his racing curricle or make the lad sprawl headlong and helpless at the worst moment. Nor did he decide a cottager's child's life was not worth risking his own and Lord Rufus Frensham's for.

Adam Lathbury had indeed paid a heavy price for his folly and she felt something hard and bitter obstruct her own breathing as she stared at him and understood his secret agony all too well. 'You need to stop wearing a hair shirt because you survived,' she told him.

'None of your business, my lady,' he said stiffly and began to pace the room.

He made her feel like a busybody, but it was better to hurt than feel nothing at all. She had tried so hard to numb her emotions when Joe died and she had to give up their baby. At least Adam Lathbury had broken through this feeling that she stood apart from the rest of the world. That piece of self-defence was dust the instant he had kissed her, and now his hurts seemed so harsh and hard they made her ache to offer him comfort or just forgetfulness, but bitter experience told her where comfort and forgetfulness led.

'Yes, it is,' she argued with him even so. 'If my actions are your business, then yours must be mine.'

'Why are you here, then?' he demanded and spun on his heel to glare a challenge at her.

'To find out where my grandmother's books and papers are so I can reclaim them.'

'I doubt if that's a good enough reason for you to come here on a night when you could so easily be caught and exposed to public scrutiny,' he argued dourly.

The reminder left a cold lump in her belly where fire and hot desire had raged such a short time ago. Good, that was how she should be, cold and hard and determined to get what she wanted without help from him.

He went back to his pacing as if it was a good excuse not to look at her. 'I suppose that list I made of the other buyers for your grandmother's collection has given you the cork-brained notion of searching their book rooms if you don't find what you really want in here,' he finally turned around and said as if he knew her that well already.

'Why would I do such an extraordinary thing?' she argued half-heartedly.

He brushed her words aside with an impatient gesture. 'Don't lie to me, Lady Melissa. We both know you are impulsive, passionate and stubborn to your very soul or you would never have come here tonight and definitely not have taken fire in my arms like that. So, unless you can put your hand on your heart and swear to me you are not all that and more, I will never believe you.'

'I have no idea how you can be so wrong,' she told him with her fingers crossed behind her back.

'Hah!'

'I have lived a very quiet life in the country until recently,' she said to remind them both she was quite capable of resisting temptation when it wasn't Lord Lathbury-shaped.

'Why? Because you thought you must pay a price for some crime you think you committed before you were hardly old enough to know what it was?' he asked her as if it was half an accusation and half inspired guesswork.

He was far too close to the truth for comfort. It *had* felt like her rightful punishment for grabbing at life and love so eagerly. It was like a harsh judgement for her sins to end up with neither Joe nor their son because she had dared to love and want a boy the conventions said she should not love or want. 'No,' she argued flatly anyway.

It wasn't a crime, it was heartbreak, her inner rebel insisted.

He went back to wearing out his fine Turkey carpet as if it was do that or try to shake the truth out of her. Try as she might to believe it was impossible, there was still this need raw and strong inside as she studied his slightly halting walk. He thought it was such a flaw, part of Limping Lord Lathbury and his broken life, and it hardly seemed like a limp at all to her.

She tried to pretend she had been looking at his fine room and crowded bookshelves as he strode towards her again. 'You have been with your eccentric grandparents for more than a decade,' he all but accused her. 'You have no idea how this wicked old world runs.'

'Oh, for goodness' sake, stop exaggerating.'

'It's true; you have no idea how to go on if you think it was a good plan to march into my library as if you own it and search for whatever you are really searching for behind my back. And look what happened,' he said with an impatient gesture at his own face as if to point out he was what happened to unwary females who invaded his space, as if that was the worst consequence he could imagine her suffering.

A silence she could not break and tell him how mistaken he was fell between them. He had brought her back to some sort of life again and that secret felt prickly and dangerous. She avoided his gaze and tried to crush the fire his kiss had lit, but it didn't even waver. She wanted him; she felt more alive than she had in over a decade. She wished in her most secret and disobedient heart that he hadn't stopped. She wanted to moan out her delight as they pushed one another to the very limits of human passion. She longed to be naked under him right now. The shocking truth was she wanted him in every way a woman could want a man.

She thought such hot need had been buried in her lost love's grave, and this uncomfortable truth wasn't at all what she wanted. She needed to be immune and cold and set only on her quest for that letter. But here it still was, a fiery need to be sensuous and alive and wanted by Adam Lathbury, a man who would never take what she wanted him to and simply walk away. A man she definitely could not have and must try her best to forget she had ever met.

'I dispute your conclusions,' she said at last, and her voice was husky with the memory of how it had felt to be close to his mighty masculine body despite that stern resolution. Didn't he know he had left her aching for more than one fiery kiss? Not from the flat challenge in his gaze to say being intimate with a ruined man was an intimacy too far. 'My grandparents visited and corresponded with the greatest thinkers of our age,' she added as if she really thought that was all this was about. 'I know more about real life than any debutante who swoons over poets and officers in scarlet coats and handsome blockheads with more hair than sense.'

'Your point being?'

'I know more than you give me credit for, Lord Lathbury.'

'Aye, from books,' he challenged as he came to a standstill far too close, as if he was daring her to deny it.

'Maybe,' she lied warily.

'Why not explore life instead of wasting your youth on dry old volumes and scholarly arguments, then?' he asked as if the idea of her cooped up in Shropshire with her maternal grandparents instead of living and loving tugged on his heartstrings.

She felt guilty because he thought she was there because of some schoolgirlish prank after her mother died. It was her cover, though, and she must maintain it. 'It was a privilege for me to live with my grandparents.'

'And you miss them sorely,' he said gently.

'Yes.'

'And now you are back with your father you must live a more conventional life?'

'Maybe.'

'Not conventional enough to join the social round, though.'

'No, not that orderly and expected, but as my father has accepted my decision it can be no business of yours what I do, Lord Lathbury.'

'Yet you are still a housebreaker and this is still my house you have broken into, Lady Melissa,' he said with a cool look to say she became his business the moment she stole in here behind his back.

'And those are still your guests such a very short distance away,' she said with a significant look in the direction of the distant-sounding music. If she kept talking about impersonal things, he might even have to return to them and leave her be. 'You are the host of a grand ball.'

'And even though I wish my guests at the devil,

it doesn't seem to dampen their enthusiasm for my hospitality.'

'Grudging or not,' she said with a wry smile at his gruff lack of enthusiasm.

'Very grudging,' he admitted and shrugged as if the joke was on him.

Chapter Six

The sound of his deep chuckle lifted her heart and she told it not to be stupid. Under the scarred recluse he still had a young man's spirit though, didn't he? Time he left his self-imposed solitude behind as well as her. The old and rash Melissa whispered, *I will if you will, my lord*, but this one knew it would be so wrong to listen to her.

'If you expect me to forget we ever met, you are going to be bitterly disappointed,' he told her as if he was already bored with his guests again and there was no point in her trying to change the subject.

'But you're a gentleman, my lord.'

'Maybe, but I'm not a fool. Promise to meet me in the Park before the fashionable crowd are out of bed tomorrow?'

'Why should I?'

'How can I help if I don't know what you need to find?'

Ah, please, no! Don't talk about need right now.

Her inner wanton was in a sensual tangle all over again at the sound of the very word on his lips and Melissa had to look away to remind herself where they were and why she was here. It had nothing to do with meeting the lord of all this scholarly splendour and everything to do with Joe and their son, she reminded herself sternly and managed to meet his challenging stare with one of her own.

'You don't need to know what I'm looking for or help find it,' she said not quite warily enough from the flare of interest in his good eye as he heard her admit she was here for something more than that list of book buyers. How could she have been so stupid?

'Now I think I do. If you would just stop and think properly—what could have happened tonight if one of the rakes had surprised you instead of me? Meet me in the Park at ten o'clock tomorrow, because if you don't I'll call on your father and ask him to explain why you broke into my house tonight instead.'

'You wouldn't dare,' she said with her heart beating so loudly she was surprised they hadn't heard it out in the ballroom and come to investigate.

'I would.'

'I won't come because you snap your fingers and order me to,' she said defensively. The temptation was still heady to break this argument and talk about the real issue—the flat truth that she still wanted him with an ache that felt all the harder to deny with every word that led them away from it. She wasn't used to being so needy and longing to know this intriguing man to the core of his soul, but he was right, it was forbidden—she wasn't the person he thought she was. That was it, then—final, set in stone and true. He was not for her and she was not for him. 'Leave me be, my lord,' she half demanded, half pleaded with him.

'If you refuse, then I am sure your father will not mind me joining him for breakfast when he realises I could let this delicious morsel of gossip about you burgling my library slip and make you a laughing stock.'

'Don't you even think about it,' she snapped as panic and betrayal and a desperate hope he was calling her bluff fought for dominance.

'Then promise to meet me,' he said implacably. She had tried her hardest to end this dangerous acquaintance but he had refused to listen.

'Very well, I promise—under extreme protest,' she said. Given a few hours' respite, she might think of a way to persuade him her quest was trivial and she had only chosen to come here tonight because she still craved excitement from time to time.

'We had best hurry now, then,' he said, reaching for her black velvet cloak even as she still stood gazing at him with her mouth open like a fool.

'Where?' she said, still all at sea even when he picked up her pistol.

'A fine piece,' he said and tested the balance of the finely wrought little pistol, 'but if you intend to go housebreaking again you should load it first.'

'I don't want to hurt anyone,' she told him. 'Or at least I didn't until I met you,' she added darkly.

A deep rumble of male laughter was no cause for

celebration, or weak knees, or wishing she was back in his arms again. 'Bad girl,' he said with a wry grin. 'Best put this on if we are going to lurk in the shadows,' he added as he held out her cloak invitingly.

'*We* are not going anywhere—*you* are going back to your guests while *I* return to my father's house alone.'

'I can deal with them later,' he said impatiently, sliding the lush velvet-and-silk-lined cape over her shoulders since she showed no sign of stepping forward to claim it. Why had it never felt this luxurious and sensual against the bare skin exposed by her evening gown before he draped it over her shoulders like a promise of more to come? 'And don't bother arguing. I won't let you walk back through mews and dark alleys alone at this time of night, Mayfair or no,' he added as if he hadn't noticed her shiver of whatever it was or her blink of startled desire.

'Oh, for goodness' sake, how do you think I got here?'

'I didn't know you then and now I do I refuse to sit and twiddle my thumbs while you take such a feather-brained risk at this time of night.'

'Wiston House is only a few hundred yards away.'

'Unless you can find a way to shoot me with an unloaded gun you can't stop me seeing you home, my lady. The sooner you get moving the sooner I'll be back to pack the last of my wearisome guests into their carriages and seek my bed.'

'Isn't it supposed to be weary instead of wearisome?'

'No,' he said tersely and tugged her into the deep

shadows on the opposite side of the room from the
door she remembered she still had the key to and hastily shoved at him. He pocketed it impatiently then
grabbed her hand again, and she was in motion before
she could protest, and of course the impatient touch
of his hand on her bare skin wasn't exciting at all.
'You're going the wrong way,' she protested rather
breathlessly all the same.

'I'm not prepared to take the risk of you being
seen by my staff.'

He paused and put out his other hand to search
among what looked like an innocent row of books.
She heard a click and a well-oiled swish of movement
and had hardly taken in the fact there had been another exit to his library all along before he towed her
out of it and down a narrow corridor leading to a side
door. He must have been finding his way by memory
since it was as dark as anywhere in this grand mansion could be on such a night. He turned the key of the
outer door as if he didn't need to look where it was,
then tugged her through it and locked it after them.

'I could have got out of that room at any time,' she
hissed in a furious whisper. The thought of the time
she spent waiting for him to come back made her feel
like a needy idiot.

'Only if you knew there was a concealed door.'

'Rat,' she accused in a fierce whisper.

'Hush!' he whispered back. What an infuriating,
overbearing, devious man he was.

It was hard to hang on to silent fury when it felt
so much safer going back than it had been stealing

through the dark byways on the way to his house, however many hours ago that was now. He was a lot bigger and stronger than she was and better at putting off furtive nightwalkers who might lurk in the shadows. And she did belong to the physically weaker sex, even if she hated that description. Never mind his limp and what he thought were infirmities, he was a powerful man, and his powerful hand in hers was sparking off all sorts of wayward wants as they stole along together like furtive lovers returning home from an assignation.

By tomorrow morning in the Park, in broad daylight, they would look back on this scandalous encounter and wonder what they ever saw in one another. Her lips tingled and other annoying parts of her she wasn't even going to think about jumped to attention and said that was a lie. Remembering how it felt to be kissed with such single-minded sensuality by such a man would not get her anywhere, though. They still crept through the dark lanes hand in hand and never mind how he felt about her as he ghosted at her side like a partner in crime.

It only took a few minutes to get through the dark lanes to Grosvenor Square and she was so contrarily disappointed Papa lived in the heart of Mayfair and not further afield that she knew she was in deep trouble. She felt as if she would gladly walk all night by His Lordship's side and never mind where he ought to be instead because she didn't want to lose the warmth of his hand in hers and this heady feeling she wasn't alone any more.

'Can you get back in without being seen?' he whispered as they stood outside the garden door, and she hesitated.

She didn't want to go in, but that was selfish. He had the last dregs of a ball to go home to. 'Of course,' she murmured crossly, because it would be folly to stay and silently beg for a kiss goodnight as if they were lovers.

'Goodnight then, termagant,' he whispered back. She was such a fool to still be smiling at his testy farewell when she let herself back in through the garden door and crept across the shadowy garden. At least this household seemed deeply asleep, so nobody was likely to hear her as she unlocked the side door with the key she had slipped into the pocket of her cloak with the pistol earlier this evening and tiptoed inside.

'Where have you been?' her father's voice whispered from the shadows. Melissa jumped and followed him into his study with a resigned sigh so they could talk without waking the household.

'I told you I was going to the opera with Betsy, Papa,' she whispered.

'Close the door behind you and speak up,' he demanded, and her suspicion he was a little bit deaf seemed to be confirmed.

'Betsy said she was going to bring me home in her carriage, so you had no need to worry about me being late, Papa.'

'I know what you told me she said, but I'm not quite the flat you think me. The opera was over hours ago and please don't try to tell me you went on somewhere sociable because I don't believe you. My daughter does not gallivant. Until tonight you didn't go out at all and I should have known it was a charade. It beats me how you thought I could calmly go to bed and sleep once I realised you were really out looking for that confounded letter your grandmother should have destroyed the moment she read it.'

Melissa watched him rub a weary hand through his shock of white hair and some of the stiffness they still felt with one another melted away. 'I'm sorry, Papa, I am such a sore trial to you,' she said with a weary gesture and a wry smile.

'Not so. I love you, Mel. Always have, always will.'

'I know,' she said. Coming back here as a truly adult woman, she realised she had seen him first through the eyes of a child, then a bitter and grieving girl who had blamed him for the loss of her baby when he had been right all along. There was no other sure way to protect her and her child from the scandal and stigma that would have haunted them for the rest of their lives if she had had her way and kept her child with her somehow. 'I love you, Papa,' she said and really meant it. 'But please can we go to bed now and talk about it in the morning?'

'Maybe, but it was all about that letter tonight, wasn't it?' he said as if he had to find out for certain before he could sleep. 'About my grandson,' he added.

There was another piece of a puzzle she had not let herself see before. 'Yes,' she admitted because he was right; this did concern him as well and he did have a grandson, somewhere, and pray God her boy was safe with his new family. 'If the truth comes out, some interfering busybody will decide it is their duty to hunt him down and visit my sins on him.'

'Aye, we live in an age of cant and sensation, and both your lives will be twisted up in it if the gossips find out about him. So how can I stand by and let it just happen to the two people I love most in the world?'

'I know you can't,' she said, and it touched her still-aching heart to hear him admit he had feelings for her son as well as his errant daughter. 'I didn't refuse to make my debut to spite you, Papa—taking my place in society would have made Joseph and our child just a couple of unfortunate slips that I could easily put aside and carry on with my life as if they never even existed.'

'I know. I suppose I was furious with the lad for leaving you alone and in a pickle at the time, but he couldn't help falling from that roof, even if he should have waited for a dry day instead of going up there in the rain when he had an impulsive young love to consider. I wanted to kill him myself when I found out you were carrying his child and you not much more than a child yourself, but I suspect it was your way of forcing my hand. You knew if you got pregnant by the lad I would have no choice but to agree to you marrying him.'

'True,' she said, and he was right, so there was no point lying. 'I did everything I could not to have to wait until we were old enough to marry without your consent. I refused to even think about waiting five years to marry the love of my life.'

'Ah, yes, my daughter the determined. Remember that wall-eyed pony you insisted on yearning after, out of all the others you could have picked?' her father said.

The relentless campaign she had waged to get her own way brought back memories of the happy family they had before her mother died. She had loved that pony with single-minded devotion and at last her parents had agreed to tolerate her choice. Yet despite being so indulged once upon a time, her relationship with her father had seemed so broken and impossible to put back together to the spoilt and impulsive girl she was at sixteen that she had put everything she had left into loving Joe.

Maybe all that heady love had felt like a heavy responsibility to a seventeen-year-old youth, she wondered as she looked back now. Perhaps he went up on that roof to reassure himself he was still a daredevil youth and not old before his time and about to be a married man. She shivered as she thought for the first time of him being so young and, yes, in love, but apprehensive about having to be a man for her sake before he was properly done with being a boy.

'But he *was* the best pony in the land, Papa,' she said with a wry smile.

'So you always insisted after you had nagged and sulked and begged us to let you have him instead of the neat one I picked out for you.'

'He never once unseated me or nipped or kicked.

He didn't walk into walls as you and Mama insisted he would before you agreed I might as well have him since I refused to even look at the one you wanted me to ride or any other.'

'Stubborn little minx,' he said with a reminiscent smile.

'True, but he was a fine pony, Papa. Joseph Briggs was a fine man as well and he would have grown up to be an even finer one if only he had lived long enough. Maybe I was a spoilt girl who went wild while your back was turned, but I really did love him with all my heart. He was my comfort and my joy when there was so very little of it in either of our lives after Mama died.'

'I should have paid you more attention, been there for you, but I was too selfish.'

'You were grieving; you had lost the love of your life.'

'And you had lost your mother; I needed horse-whipping for leaving you to struggle with such a terrible loss alone while I brooded and drank and refused to see you because you are so much like her that it hurt. She would have been so furious with me for that; I'm surprised she hasn't come back to haunt me.'

'You would welcome it if she did.'

'I might not if she was as tempestuously angry with me as I think she would have been for neglecting her daughter when you needed me most. Maybe that's why she doesn't haunt me, perhaps that's my punishment.'

'Oh, Papa, no. She loved you too much to punish

you for loving her too much,' she said and raised her hand to smooth it gently down his cheek as he looked as if he was about to weep for the loss of her mother even now. 'And I understand. I know how it feels. I longed for Joe so much after he died that I used to pray I would die as well.'

'Thank God you didn't, my Mel,' he said shakily.

'Finding out I was carrying his baby stopped me doing anything reckless and I don't think I was quite sane after he died. We had only just found out how much we loved one another and then he was gone, between one breath and the next. The world was so dark and blank without him that I really do understand how you felt when Mama died now.'

'Maybe you do, but I don't deserve that understanding. You lived for your child and I just ignored mine.'

'For a while, but you did what I needed you to when I wasn't capable of rational thought and saved my child from leading a miserable life. If you had let me cling to him, he would have had to fight being born illegitimate from the cradle to the grave. Now I see how other ladies' bastards are treated I shudder. You were right; I had to give him up so he could have a better life than I could give him and I know you found him good parents.'

Melissa wondered if feeling alive again was such a good thing as tears threatened to flow from her tired eyes. She felt as if she was saying goodbye to a wonderful dreamland where Joe had lived and they would have had several more children by now to run about with their eldest brother and never mind if their mother was supposed to be a lady.

'But that's enough of the past, Papa. It's late and you look even more tired than I am.'

'Aye, I am, but that brings us back to where you came in—where were you?'

'Doing my duty as a mother,' she admitted on a weary sigh. 'And don't argue you could have gone in my stead because you are too well known not to be caught red-handed.'

'Did you find anything I could not have done as easily by asking?'

'Yes, I discovered who bought Grandmama's books and papers. I have a list of buyers that I intend to keep to myself so you can't decide to do this for me.'

'You insist I am too conspicuous.'

'And you know as well as I do that I didn't get all my quirks and impulsiveness from Mama's side of the family, so stop trying to pretend I did.'

'How can I leave you to it when you are looking for something that should never have been left about for anyone to find in the first place?'

'I still don't understand what came over Grandmama to do such a thing, but there we are, it did and now I must deal with it.'

'Not alone.'

'No,' she agreed, and she really wasn't alone with this problem. There was something of a crowd with Lord Lathbury wanting to pile into the fray alongside her father. 'Now do let's go to bed, Papa, it's *long* after my bedtime.'

He chuckled at the childhood rebuke to his over-lively daughter and agreed it was high time they both got some sleep.

Chapter Seven

Melissa thought it was going to be impossible to sleep after her eventful evening and was astonished when she woke up to see bright sunlight peeping through a gap in the shutters. That clock couldn't possibly be right, she decided and blinked, then looked again. Lathbury said she was to meet him at ten o'clock or he would come here instead and it was half past nine already! She jumped out of bed and rang the bell, then ran into her dressing room, cursing herself for sleeping so deeply.

'Wretched, wretched man, what right does he have to dictate where I go and when?' None at all, of course, but the last thing she wanted was him coming here.

'Oh, lawks, my lady, you're already up and washed.' Her maid interrupted Melissa's frantic hurry to get dressed and out of the house in the shortest time possible.

'I'm in a hurry, Ellen.'

'I can see that, Your Ladyship. You're making a

rat's nest of your hair and your stays need fastening properly before you throw that old thing over them any old how.'

'You do it, then, but I have to be out of the house in ten minutes.'

'I don't know if I've ever seen you in such a tear to get out in the world.'

'And this is you hurrying?' Melissa muttered from behind the heavy curtain of hair Ellen had insisted on brushing despite her protests it could do without just this once.

'If you stop arguing, we'll be done all the quicker,' Ellen said with exaggerated patience.

Melissa sighed and wondered when she had become so helpless she could no longer dress herself. Still, this was London and she was vain enough to want to be presentable for this appointment with the man who had kissed her breathless last night. She tried hard not to remember how delicious it felt to be kissed by a powerful and fully mature adult male, but her heart thundered at the memory and it took all her willpower not to touch her needy mouth as if his had just left it.

No! She couldn't want gruff, defensive and stubborn Lord Lathbury so urgently it was like a constant prickle of heat under her skin, she chided herself, but hot need raged defiantly inside her anyway. None of the reasons she lined up to convince her rebel body it couldn't have him seemed to stop her feeling so different since she had met him that she hardly recognised her own face in the dressing mirror and hastily turned her gaze away.

'There, now sit down again and we'll soon be done,' Ellen said tersely.

Her maid expertly flipped a gown over Melissa's newly dressed hair, and she glanced in the mirror again as she stood up like an automaton for Ellen to button up the dove grey pelisse suitable for half-mourning because she knew perfectly well her own fingers were not up to the task. Trying for some sort of rational thought to cling to in a newly puzzling world, Melissa decided soft grey quieted down her embarrassing hair much better than last night's dark rose silk, but it was the only fashionable evening gown that had been delivered so far.

She caught herself drifting into a reverie of watching Lord Lathbury spellbound by her in her latest new outfit. She felt so out of sorts with herself that she tied the ribbons of her new bonnet so punishingly tight that Ellen clicked her tongue.

'You'll scratch your face on the straw, my lady,' her maid said as she undid and retied the ribbons. 'You're clearly not yourself this morning and I hope he's worth it,' the woman said with a sly smile and a nod at the relentlessly ticking clock as if to say wasn't she in a hurry?

'So do I,' Melissa muttered and didn't bother to rebuke an old friend when it would only make her sure she was right about the man she was in fluster about. Her son *was* worth it, though. Lathbury might be, if not for the fact she had a son. So, this was only a matter of business. No reason to panic or feel as if she was perched on the edge of a precipice and in danger of stepping off into thin air.

'You are fashionably late, my lady.'

Adam put his watch back in his pocket and raised his eyebrows. Flustered and ruffled from hurrying to their rendezvous, she was even more breathtaking in broad daylight than she had been in candlelight. He had hoped she would seem less fascinating in the merciless light of an April morning, but she had disappointed him. Sunlight picked out intriguing gold and chestnut lights in her fiery hair and showed off the flawless creamy skin he wanted to explore inch by tempting inch until he knew her inside and out.

How he wished he could rid her of every stitch of the silvery grey outfit she probably thought subdued her bright hair, when it only made him want to snatch off her bonnet and unloose its beauty to the April breeze, then get her somewhere they could remove the rest of it with undue haste before they outraged the few park-keepers and early strollers abroad at this unfashionable hour of the day.

'I was debating with myself whether to stroll round to Wiston House and see if your father is at home to visitors this morning,' he lied. If he told her what he was really thinking about, she would probably run all the way back to Shropshire and bury herself in the country for another decade.

'I'm here now and it's only ten past ten,' she said with a resentful look that made him want to kiss her into a better humour, or maybe he had best enjoy the challenge of watching her in a bad one as they were in a public place. At least the fashionable crowds who would flock here in a few hours' time to see and be seen were not even out of bed yet, and he had better not think about beds any more.

'I take it you aren't at your best of a morning?' he managed to say smoothly—there were advantages to once having been a dashing young baron after all.

'Certainly not on this one,' she muttered with a dour look to say she would like it a lot better without him.

'You did have a late night and are probably not used to breaking and entering and sneaking round strange houses for goodness knows what reason.'

'It wasn't an entertainment,' she told him resentfully, and, as she clearly had no idea her testiness was more temptation to kiss her sweet lips again, he couldn't accuse her of coquettishness.

There was something far too straightforward and brave about her and she had upended his preconceptions of what women expected of a man like him. He badly wanted to find out more and not frighten her back into her shell again, so he must bite down on this need to kiss her witless and not arguing with his wickedest intentions and behave himself.

'Really?' he said. 'It felt like a party to me and from the look of my weary servants this morning I believe they thought so, too.'

'You know perfectly well that's not what I mean and you seem far too cheerful after a night like that.'

'Ah, but I have good reason to be cheerful because last night I met you.'

'Bah!' she said, and he was delighted. She had forgotten to hide her true spirit behind the blankly enquiring look and pretend coolness. He ought to be serious and forget how much brighter his world had been since he kissed her and she kissed him. But he had enjoyed every last second of it and some things were unforgettable.

'I assure you it was a great honour to be the first man to lay eyes on the reclusive Lady Melissa Aldercombe in more than a decade.'

'That's not all you laid on me,' she told him crossly, then looked annoyed with herself for reminding them both they had kissed like lovers last night. 'Now look what you made me do,' she accused him, with such a fierce frown that he reached to smooth it out before he remembered they were in public.

He was pretty sure nobody had seen that giveaway gesture of intimacy and he snatched his hand away as if she had burned him. She did start at his touch, as if she felt the charge of something elemental sparking between them at the slightest contact as well, then she shook her head like an irritated cat with her fur being rubbed the wrong way.

'And you exaggerate; I met gentlemen under my grandparents' roof and when we visited friends, so I am not as reclusive as you make out.'

'Most of Mr and Mrs Granger's friends must have been elderly and I doubt many of them could see you that well after a lifetime poring over their books.'

'Just like you, then,' she said, then seemed to remind herself she was supposed to be a cool and controlled female who didn't much care what anyone thought of her. A pity, he decided as he watched her put fetters on her temper. 'That was rude; I apologise,' she said distantly and with her eyes on the horizon.

It was his turn to frown. 'I prefer plain dealing to a refusal to say anything significant lest it comes back to bite you.'

'In your shoes I would be grateful I am too polite to say what I really think, Lord Lathbury,' she told him, and he grinned and held out his arms as if offering her a free shot at his person with whatever weapon she had handy.

'For heaven's sake, call me Adam, Melissa. I cannot endure all this *my lord* this and *my lady* that nonsense with all these secret meetings stacking up around us to make such rigid formality look like folly.'

'No, the folly would be in encouraging an intimacy that will bite like an asp if it ever comes out, my lord. You have a little sister and I have my own reasons to avoid scandal. We are the merest acquaintances who met by chance last night.'

'What are your reasons, then?' he asked, carefully ignoring that last sentence doing its best to set them at a stony distance from one another, and he couldn't oblige her and fade meekly into the background. It would paint his world black and white again instead of these rich colours—like an etching of a great painting that should glow with colour and depth, but was a mere suggestion of itself in print. He felt sick and oddly vulnerable as he thought about his life before she had stolen into his house last night and showed him what he was missing.

'Private,' she said starkly, and her mouth set in that stubborn line he was beginning to be very familiar with.

'Very much so if they are why you cut yourself off from the world when you should have been too young and foolish to have secrets worth keeping,' he said, and jealousy suddenly took the edge off his curiosity.

What if her grand secret was another man? She could be some lucky devil's secret wife or forbidden love for all he knew. The very idea left him feeling hollow, but she would have rebuffed him last night if she owed her loyalty to someone else. Somehow he knew she would keep a promise, however dearly it cost her, and he was hardly temptation incarnate so she must be free.

'Well, they are,' she said.

'They are what?' He struggled to remember what they were talking about before he tortured himself with that notion—her reason for avoiding polite society, he recalled now.

'Private. My reasons for not making my debut or joining the *ton* since are my own to keep. I have the right to privacy, my lord,' she said with a look halfway between puzzlement and exasperation, and it made him want to kiss her all over again.

He struggled with the certainty he would still want her if she had half a dozen secret husbands and a lover or two on the side. 'True, but we are going round in circles and I thought you didn't want me to demand an interview with you in the open, so to speak.'

He had come here meaning to persuade her to carry on looking for whatever she was looking for with his help. He had begun with honourable intentions towards her, but her presence subverted them. Now he just wanted to see her again until she was as knotted up in desire as he was, and what did that make him? Best not to know, he told himself grimly.

'I don't,' she confirmed with a stubborn set to her delicious mouth that made it look even more kissable.

'Then tell me what you are up to before I send my visiting card every day until your father agrees to see me. This way is quicker and will prevent gossip.'

'As if you care about that,' she said scornfully.

'I do care. I have a sister's reputation to worry about as well as yours this Season.'

'Then consider hers and let me worry about mine, Lord Lathbury,' she said, and something dark and painful under her flat words made him want to hold her until she forgot past, present and future in his arms. Best not, at least not in the middle of Hyde Park with time marching on round them.

'I can't do that, my lady,' he told her. He was in too deep to let her search every private library that might hold her grandmother's papers without him.

'Why ever not?'

'Because you're not very good at it and heaven knows what you'll get up to behind my back.'

'My business and my risk,' she said curtly, as if

she really thought he would shrug and walk away as if she didn't matter.

'You made it mine last night.'

'Because you were bored and uncomfortable, and quizzing me seemed better than returning to your guests and playing the good host. That's not an acceptable reason to interfere in a lady's life, my lord.'

'It is for me. For now it will be enough if we walk back to Grosvenor Square as if we are nothing more than polite acquaintances strolling in the same direction. At this hour of the day we may be forgiven the lack of a maid or footman if we manage to get you home before the polite world sees us.'

'My father's servants have enough to do without running about after me.'

'This is London; you need one with you and it will make you conspicuous if you refuse to bend to the rules of polite behaviour.'

'If you say so,' she said as if she intended to do whatever she wanted never mind what he said.

'I do and I used to be an expert on staying just the right side of the line not to have to marry a society beauty. You should take my advice if you don't want to have to wed me to save us a scandal.'

'You sound as if you were a devil with the ladies once upon a time, my lord. Is that what you are trying to do with me?' A short pause while he glared at her for taking his advice so lightly. 'Make me your flirt,' she explained as if she didn't even care, and it hurt.

'I am not flirting with you and the truth is I don't

know what I am doing with you. You are a complete mystery to me, Lady Melissa.'

'Good.'

'Whatever we are or are not we must walk before the fashionable throng turn up for their ritual exercise and find us here before them and still arguing.'

'I suppose so,' she said suspiciously. He could have provided a long list of all the things he would like to do to shock the fashionable throng to their sophisticated marrow, but decided it wasn't the time or place to let her know she had all his attention and a bit more he hadn't even known he had until he met her.

Chapter Eight

With a loud sigh to let him know she was doing so reluctantly, Melissa laid the very tips of her fingers on the crook of Lord Lathbury's mockingly offered arm. Even with her gloves and his impeccable dark blue superfine coat sleeve and all the rest of his gentlemanly attire between her and his powerful body, she was so aware of him it was difficult to hear what he was saying for a fuzzy moment, as if her body had been waiting for a lover like him for so long it was determined to have him by hook or by crook.

'I'm sorry about my limp,' he said gruffly. It wasn't even a trick to make her look at him, so she could hardly lose her temper when he wasn't even trying to disarm her.

'I'm sorry about it, too, but I can't imagine why you feel you need to apologise for it,' she said lightly, as if it was no great matter—except it obviously mattered to him.

'It was my fault, but never mind my youthful follies; we have more important things to discuss. Like your youthful follies and whatever secret you are so determined to keep.'

'I am?' she said with a weary sigh, disappointed he refused to talk about his accident and was trying to fog the issue with things *she* didn't want to talk about.

'Yes, you are,' he said as if he wanted to shake the truth out of her but was far too much of a gentleman. Now there was temper and what looked like hurt in his eye because she refused to confide in him. Hurting him felt so wrong she was in danger of telling him things she didn't want him to know, and that would never do.

'Why does it matter to you?' she countered after a street of silently pacing at his side to prove she wasn't intimidated.

'Because you can't steal into Spilling's study or Mayburn's library on the next dark night and ransack their collections without being caught red-handed,' he said, and it did sound impossible when he put it like that.

'I have to,' she argued anyway.

'Not on your own.'

'Yes, exactly on my own. There's no other way.'

'There is. I'll come with you.'

'No, it's impossible for Lord Lathbury to creep into gentlemen's private residences after dark and search through their libraries. Your good name would be in ruins and how do you think your grandmother would feel if she had to bail you out of the nearest lock-up?'

'*My* good name? What about yours? If you refuse

to worry about that, think of your father's position in the Cabinet if you are caught pillaging a stranger's book collection in the middle of the night.'

'He knows I have a good reason.'

'So good you refuse to tell me what it is even though you think it would make me give up on you and go away? Do you intend telling the constables why you have been caught breaking into a gentleman's residence at midnight? No, I can see that you don't. I believe you would hang first, Lady Melissa.'

Would she? She considered such a grim end to her quest and maybe he was right. Best not think too deeply about the consequences of being caught housebreaking when she must risk it at least twice more. Her father's influence would probably get her imprisoned instead of condemned to death, or maybe even released into his custody and written off as truly mad instead of just rumoured to be so when she was younger. Adam might have made her think harder than she wanted to about what she was doing, but she still had to do it.

'It would not be a secret if I went around telling everyone,' she made herself say lightly.

The very idea of carrying on with her quest at peril of her life made her so tense she gripped his arm far too tightly for her words to be plausible. She forced herself to relax her fingers until her hold on him was fingertip-deep, as befitted strangers in company. It felt so right to snuggle her hand into the crook of his arm as if it belonged, when it was not locked in his own larger one, or making mischief with his superbly

tailored coat, or… Best stop there. Her wicked imagination would get her into even more trouble if she
wasn't careful.

'I am not everyone,' he said curtly and sounded
impatient because she was trying to make him a
stranger again for his own good.

If he took it to heart, he might avoid her in the future and stop trying to interfere, but somehow that
didn't feel like the right outcome. It felt the loneliest
one imaginable and she had been so lonely for so long.
She was going to miss him so much when he gave up
on her. She felt the gap he would leave like a physical
ache and was tempted to cling like a vine.

Instead she walked as upright and aloof as a
woman could with her fingertips tingling from the
temptation of a strong male so close all it took was
a stronger grip to show him she wanted more touch,
more intimacy and a lot more privacy. She hadn't
even known him for a full day yet and he felt crucial to her well-being, as if he was imprinted on her
mind for good and no amount of wishing would ever
remove him.

Looking back at the last decade, she pitied her
stern isolation from most of her own kind from here
even if she was going to have to let him go. At the
time it had felt like fit punishment for something she
wasn't sure she was even guilty of with hindsight.
Love, she supposed, guilty of loving recklessly and
fully, blindly believing the future was hers and Joe's
when Fate had other plans.

A stern reminder you could believe you had everything you ever wanted at your fingertips and Fate would shut them in the door while busy slamming it in your face. You would be on the other side of it and so starkly alone it felt better not to have loved at all. And this stupid feeling that Adam Lathbury would be uniquely hers if Fate was kinder only made her more sure than ever she had to make him go away.

'True,' she managed to say coolly enough, 'but I'm still not telling you.'

'I can keep a secret as close as the grave, Melissa.'

He probably could as well. He had once been a handsome young rake and kept quiet about his amours, so rumour was right—he was a discreet and dashing lover until the accident marred his looks. She didn't think much of rumour or his former lovers for letting such lies about his desirability, or lack of it, afterwards circulate.

Adam had listened to it; he thought the marks from his accident on his face and body were his punishment, and perhaps the polite world took their cue from him, so the myth perpetuated in a weary cycle she fiercely wanted to break. The way he set his jaw and controlled his sensitive, sensuous mouth, the braced set of his shoulders when he thought someone was about to find him hideous, only fed the lie.

She wanted to kick the silly girls who had shied away from him last night as if he was a monster when he was nothing of the kind. She shot a sidelong glance at him. Even in daylight, with just a fine top hat to shade his damaged face from the eyes of the world, he still looked like a haughty pirate to her. Desire still ran so hot and dizzy under her skin she had to look away again or latch on to him like that vine and beg for the nearest privacy to climb all over him to their mutual satisfaction. What were they talking about? Ah, yes, secrets. The reason she was never going to do anything of the kind.

'I shall not burden you with any more of them, my lord, and I did not give you permission to use my given name,' she made herself say.

'Very well, Lady.'

'That's not what I meant and you know it.'

'There really is no pleasing you this morning.'

'It will be time for the *ton* to be abroad again if we don't hurry up.'

'True, we don't want the fashionable hordes wondering who the mysterious beauty on the Limping Lord's arm is, do we?'

'No, we don't, and stop worrying about the idiots who christened you that. They aren't worth a snap of your fingers,' she told him brusquely.

'Even so I would rather we were out of sight before they are out and about, Lady Melissa.'

'Very well, my lord. Is there anything else you would like to order me to do, my lord?' she teased him, because she couldn't bear watching the vulnerability of his surprisingly sensitive mouth when he stopped being on his guard. How wonderful life would be for a woman who *could* show him he was more attractive for having once been broken and come out stronger.

'Well, if you don't know by now, Lady Melissa, I

quite despair of your intellect and native wit,' he said with what must be Beau Lathbury's smooth manner of old and, meeting his wicked gaze, she realised how dangerous that bold young lord must have been.

'Stop it,' she ordered. 'You are a very infuriating man.'

'I almost made you laugh though, didn't I?'

'Maybe,' she said, doing her best not to smile as his act of the piratical would-be seducer warmed another of the cold places in her heart.

'Before we end up back where you began this rash and perilous expedition, we must plan our next one,' he said.

Glory, but he was stubborn, wasn't he? 'I am going home for my breakfast and an afternoon in my father's library instead of yours. That is all I plan to do today and all you need to know.'

'You can't brush me off so easlly. I won't let you.'

'Papa will be very shocked to find you in his library instead of your own, then, my lord,' she managed to say as if the thought of him dogging her every step didn't make her feel heavy limbed and wistful.

'Stop it, Melissa. I am not going to be fobbed off or go away meekly as a kicked lapdog. I am certainly not going to leave you fumbling about the country looking for this secret of yours alone. You are slender and smaller than either of the men who bought the other papers and books, and you can't fight them off if they attack you. How will you find what you want and escape their lairs without my help? You were so absorbed in your reading last night the crack of doom could have sounded and you wouldn't have heard it.'

'Don't be ridiculous,' she said with a dismissive gesture to say he was being melodramatic. Secretly she loved the idea he would worry about her out there without him to make jeopardy into an intriguing game. 'I promise to load my pistol if it makes you feel better.'

'Of course it doesn't. Shooting a respectable householder while burgling his home will only get you hanged all the sooner.'

'If I had shot you last night, at least I could plead extreme provocation.'

'If you had shot me, I wouldn't be here to care what idiocy you are planning next.'

'Don't,' she said, suddenly finding this joke far too serious as she thought of Joe and how appalling losing another man in the blink of an eye would feel. Her life would be even more cold and lonely and bereft than it was last time if he died as well, she decided. So this entanglement had clearly had to stop. She must end it before they got too close and she lost everything all over again.

If she allowed herself the pleasure of his company too often, they would both end up hurting and he had been hurt too much already. 'Why do you need to know what I am looking for?' she asked carefully, hoping her question would make him think harder about his insistence on being involved in a felony and take a step back.

'So I can help you look for it, of course.'

'Why? Why do you need to know?'

He seemed flummoxed by her question and they strolled into Grosvenor Square in silence. She blessed her guardian angel for keeping it empty of curious pedestrians or even any early visitors to the other grand houses in the Square.

'I suppose I don't need to know more than that you are looking for something, although it would be hard for me to help you search for it without knowing what it is,' he said at last.

'Just let me into your library and show me where the books and papers you bought from my grandmother's library are kept so I can look through them. That will be an end to the matter as far as you are concerned, and you will know if I find it or not.'

'My staff would be mighty surprised if the mysterious Lady Melissa Aldercombe marched up the steps and demanded admittance to my library,' he said far too lightly, but she could tell he had not given up on the idea of joining in her later adventures if he didn't have what she was looking for from the stubborn set of his chin.

'I would come to the side door we left by last night and you could let me in without them knowing I was there, Lord Lathbury.'

'Adam,' he corrected her with a frown.

'No.'

'Lathbury, then—at least there isn't a "my lord" in it.'

'You are impossible, my lord.'

'Said the pot to the kettle, and what time shall I

expect you to meet me outside your father's house tonight?'

'I proved I could look after myself by getting into your house unnoticed last night.'

'I will come in with you now and invite your father instead, then, shall I? I am sure we men can get this business done without you and at least I won't have to marry him if we are caught together in my library late at night.'

'Don't you dare involve him, tonight or on any other night, if you don't have the item I am looking for.'

'Meet me at the garden door of Wiston House tonight, then, and I won't have to hang around waiting for you to come out,' he said impatiently. 'I'm far too old and too distinctive to get away with playing the back-door Romeo.'

He would be mocked and lampooned if an outsider found out he was helping her search for proof of the scandal that would be her undoing. Adam was too sensitive about his injuries already to be held up for mockery because of her, and she hated the very idea of it.

'Why take such a risk for a stranger, then? You hadn't even met me this time yesterday,' she said, and maybe she wanted him to argue they didn't feel like strangers to him either.

'Maybe I'm an interfering idiot,' he said with a wry smile.

'How I wish you were,' she muttered glumly.

'That's not nice, Melissa, and you could just think

of me as your partner in crime if it makes you feel better.'

'It doesn't, and it's not a crime to recover something my cousin had no right to sell in the first place.'

'I suppose if you demand them back openly my fellow bibliophiles would immediately decide to search through them to find what the fuss is about.'

'Indeed,' she said. Scholars *were* curious; it was in their make-up. As soon as one of them read any letter from that time in her life the cat would be out of the bag.

'Eleven o'clock, then,' he said, and she looked at him blankly. 'Most working people will be in bed by then and even if the *ton* is still rattling about we can hide in a dark corner until they have gone by.'

'Are neither of us ever to sleep again of a night?'

'Apparently not, but you started it. Now, here we are, back at Wiston House again, and it's high time you went in if you want to maintain your precious seclusion, Lady Melissa. The fashionable throng will begin to flutter out of doors like the social butterflies they are very soon now. We could always join them if you have changed your mind about avoiding them altogether, I suppose, but I warn you it will cause a sensation and you will be mobbed with callers every day until the end of the Season.'

'You know I haven't changed my mind,' she told him with a shudder and a frustrated glare at him as she thought of such an onslaught and knew it was his fault she couldn't bring herself to tell him abruptly to just leave her alone and march away with her nose in the air. Because she didn't want to part with him like that, they had taken this risky, tempting and far too slow walk home. Not that he would have been so easily shaken off, she decided darkly and shot him another glower in case he'd missèd the first one.

'Are you going in, then,' he said as if he had no idea she was trying her hardest to be furious with him, 'or do I now have to call on your father and ask him to search my share of those books and papers in your stead?'

'No, leave him alone,' she said crossly and saw a smug smile kick up his firm mouth. They both knew he held all the cards in this trick. The whole match was still to play for and she would outfox him yet. 'Oh, very well,' she conceded as they stood outside her father's house and risked the neighbours' curiosity. 'If you insist on interfering in my private affairs, I shall have no choice but to meet you tonight.'

'I do,' he said, so blandly composed she wanted to shake him.

'I will be there,' she said with a very audible sigh to let him know he was being ungentlemanly as well as very annoying.

'And don't be late this time. I am far too conspicuous to take up lurking quietly in doorways with my limp and eyepatch.'

'I will *not* be late,' she murmured between clenched teeth, then gave him a brisk nod of farewell before running up the steps of Wiston House. The door opened for her before she got there.

'His Grace wishes to speak with you, my lady,'

the butler told her solemnly, and Melissa wondered if she would ever break her fast today. Perhaps she would still be faint with hunger when she stole out to meet Adam tonight and have to cling to him like a vine all the way to his house after all.

His misplaced humour seemed to be rubbing off on her, she decided, as she removed her fine kid gloves and new bonnet before smoothing a curl back into place and inspecting her reflection in a nearby mirror. Hmm, there was a flush on her cheeks, and her eyes looked brighter than they had been since her grandmother died. She tweaked another stray curl into place and nodded sternly at her reflection to remind herself life was serious and Adam Lathbury was not for her.

'You are very quiet tonight, Adam.'

'Am I, darling? Then put it down to ennui after the drama and excitement we stirred up last night,' Adam told his grandmother, thankful she had no idea how much drama and excitement his part of yesterday evening contained.

'If I can do all that at my age and not feel any ill effects the next day, then I don't see why you cannot shrug off one late night at yours.'

'Ah, but you are ageless and invincible, don't forget. You told me so when I wanted to ask my cousin Lavinia to stay and share the flitting about you and Belle are set on this Season so you can take a rest now and again.'

'Ridiculous idea—you know very well I detest her.

She sniffs all the time, and as for that pug she insists on taking everywhere, I don't wonder she sniffs with such a stink under her nose all the time. I know I would if I had to endure his company for very long, or hers for that matter.'

'Poor Cousin Lavinia.'

'Humbug. I never could abide your mama's sister, and the girl is the spit of her mother. Lavinia wants to marry you; we can't have that.'

'No, we definitely can't,' Adam said with a shudder at the very idea of ending up wed to his cousin and her smelly pug.

'Inbreeding,' the Dowager Lady Lathbury explained very bluntly.

Adam had a job not to splutter soup everywhere when he caught his little sister's eye and Belle rolled hers in silent amusement. Thank goodness his little sister had not grown up a prude, although she stood very little chance of doing so with their grandmother on hand to nip any signs of missishness in the bud.

'And you would end up strangling the woman.'

'Cousin Lavinia obviously will not do, then. But is there nobody you trust to chaperon Belle now and again?'

'I ain't in my dotage, my boy, but Tilly Cranford would do if we ever need her to take my place. In the meantime Belle and I are quite happy as we are.'

'We dare not be anything else when you have been to so much trouble to keep our cousin and Pug away, Grandmama,' Belle said.

'Impudent girl—and you still ain't said what it is

you're stewing over, my lad,' his grandmother went on as if she was determined not to be distracted.

'Nothing. Not being as invincible as you are, I dare say I am just tired.'

'Taken all those silly chits' bad behaviour last night to heart, if you ask me—no bottom, these modern girls.'

'Some of them looked to have a trifle too much of a one as they scurried away from me at speed last night.'

Now it was Belle's turn to splutter and put her spoon down before she risked taking another mouthful. 'You two are quite outrageous. Don't you know I am supposed to be a delicately nurtured female? It should be your duty to set me a good example.'

'Fustian,' his grandmother said grandly, but Adam decided to ignore the look of genuine concern she shot him, as if she really thought he had been hurt by the reaction of a pack of unfledged girls to his marred face.

He was surprised to discover it all seemed rather amusing with hindsight. He doubted it would have been before he found Lady Melissa Aldercombe hiding in his library to make the ball a mere sideshow to the main event of his evening. 'So where are the two of you intent on gadding off to tonight?' he asked, since he needed to plan his next unusual evening with Melissa Aldercombe around them.

He wanted and liked the woman, but he wasn't sure he could stomach being married to her if they were caught together. A marriage of convenience, even with a woman who could look him in the face and not flinch, would be cold and dutiful, and there was nothing dutiful or cold about his hot desire to bed Lady Melissa from the moment he first laid eyes on her. But he didn't see how she could ever love a beast like him and he didn't know what love was anyway.

He had thought he loved Dorinda Merriot five years ago, but it turned out to be an illusion. After Dorinda had erased him from her life since he no longer fitted her picture of perfection—and who could blame her?—he had decided if that was love he had been lucky to escape it without too much harm on either side.

There was something unique about Lady Melissa that argued loving her would never be easy on either of them, or as lightly forgotten when it ended as it surely must with him being him and her being her. She had an ardent heart under the wary coolness she tried to use to keep the world at bay and she deserved far more from life than she seemed to think she did.

His instincts said she should have everything she had denied herself until now—love, passion, security and a family of her own. He certainly wasn't anywhere close to being that sort of everything for any woman now. So, he must help her find what she was looking for and then stand aside for the better man she would be able to find when this mysterious secret of hers was safe.

The thought of him joining Her Ladyship in the marital bed between their quarrels and misadventures, instead of the perfect Adonis she probably deserved, was just an erotic fairy tale he told himself in idle moments like this one when his imagination ran wild before he could haul it back to face reality.

She was a mature and desirable woman and he wasn't made of ice, so of course he wanted her, and why wouldn't he? He was a mature and not very desirable man, but there was something about Melissa's bravery and the fiery nature under all that wary restraint she tried so hard to cling to that made him want a better life for her than she had now.

Somehow he must keep his hands off her and protect her from all the other bookish wolves until this secret of hers was safe. Then he would walk away and leave her to find a gallant gentleman she could love and respect and spend the rest of her life with. He just hoped he didn't run mad before they got her secret back or embarrass them both by begging for what he knew he couldn't have—her in his bed, eager and fiery and unrestrained as nature intended.

Chapter Nine

'You are late this time,' Melissa whispered crossly as Adam sauntered into view and she slid out of the shadows to meet him.

'Not late, fashionably on time,' he bent forward to argue with her softly. A frisson of heady excitement shivered through to her very toes as he whispered in her ear, and that wasn't why they were here.

The mere idea of meeting him for a late-night tryst felt seductive and so exciting her stupid heart was racing and her insides felt molten, but she squashed the temptation to lean into him and encourage delicious intimacy and maybe a sweet slow kiss in the dark.

'Late, in other words,' she said grumpily even as awareness of him as a potent male snaked down her backbone and reached places she had been trying to ignore for years.

'An old friend called and I thought he'd never leave. I had to yawn and lie about being worn out from the ball to get here now, so please stop nagging me about it since someone will come out to see what's going on out here if we don't leave soon.'

Melissa knew he was right, so she let him tug her into the shadows and steal off into the night because it was best to get this over with and not because he was a superior male who thought he could throw orders at her like a general in battle. Yet she did feel safe, and something deeper and darker than simple friendship or kindness to a stranger ran beneath this odd sense of familiarity she had with him and she wasn't sure she wanted to know what it really was.

She had known Joe so well before that never-to-be-forgotten day when fire and wonder flared between them and love fell into her life fully formed. He had been her best friend long before he was her lover. From that moment on Joe was her touchstone, her lost lover, her only love and the life she was never going to have once she lost him.

So, her feelings for this very different man were nothing like the strongest and truest certainty she had—that when she had loved Joseph he had truly loved her back. He was her one and only love and that was that. This was lust; it had to be. If she felt the same fire, the same driven desire burning inside her for this man she had only known for a day, it could make what she had with Joe seem less and that was impossible.

Yet here she was, hand in hand with Adam Lathbury, and his strong hand in hers felt as familiar as if they had been meeting palm to palm like this for years. Everything about him disturbed her and she still couldn't make herself let go and insist she could manage without his touch perfectly well. She could walk alone, as she had done for a decade. Or she could leave it where it wanted to be as his heat melded with her heat and she hardly knew where one stopped and the other began in this heady darkness with her senses so overloaded with him even the sooty night air smelt sharp and exciting.

She didn't want to want him, but a hum of sensual awareness ran through her like wildfire all the same. She reminded herself where hot desire led and why she was here. Yet he still dominated her senses and thoughts until she was astonished nobody else knew he was creeping through mews and alleys at her side, so she didn't have to do it alone. She was so conscious of his powerful body moving next to her she could have picked him out from a vast crowd of humanity just from the prickle of heady awareness that threatened to flame out of control if this furtive journey took an instant longer than it should.

Last night she had crept along this path alone in the shadows and Adam Lathbury was just one more man she didn't want to meet. Tonight she had to remind herself he was a stranger who might have something she wanted so badly it should put anything else out of her head.

Yes, that was it, the stern reminder she needed. It was her job as a mother to find that letter her grandmother had had about her and destroy it. What if it wasn't among Adam's books and papers from the sale? What if she had to get inside two more large houses? The idea of doing it without him seemed stark and terrifying, but she would manage it. She had been coping alone since she bid that heartbroken farewell to her baby. She was so used to being alone it almost felt safe and that was as well. The sooner she got on with her life without Adam Lathbury in it the better.

'Hush,' Adam ordered his silent companion as they reached the side door of his house.

He could actually feel her fury with him through their joined hands. He wondered why she thought she could fool anyone she was cool and aloof when she was the exact opposite, and that was a very good reason to keep her wanting to be both when a goodly part of him certainly didn't.

Once they were inside he led the way and refused to let her turn him into a meek follower in my lady's angry wake. There was another thing he marvelled she didn't know about herself—she was a duke's daughter to her fingertips when she was angry or offended, or both. And he wanted the haughty minx as much as the fierce lioness or the passionate lover who had taken light in his arms last night. No—that Lady Melissa was the best and worst of them all. So, he had to get control of all this wanting before they were back in the light and she could see how rampant being so close to her in the dark had made him.

'At last,' he murmured once the hidden door was shut behind them and he could let go of her hand and the temptation to touch all those Melissas all over if only she would let him. He must recall his sane and sensible resolution to help her find what she wanted and leave her to live her life. He limped over to light a taper from the single candle left burning again and set it to the makings of a fire already on the hearth.

'Where are they?' she interrupted his reverie impatiently.

He turned to look at her, then blinked and shook his head and looked again. He wrenched his gaze away as desire whipped through him like a lightning bolt. 'What the devil are you doing out and about dressed like that?' he barked, forgetting he was supposed to be as quiet as the proverbial mouse in his own town house so that nobody would know His Lordship was definitely not alone in his library tonight.

'Waiting to be told where my grandmother's books and papers are before I look through them, hopefully find what I am looking for and go back where I came from as swiftly as possible,' she said with exaggerated patience, as if she had no idea why he was glaring at the corner of his own book room as if it was his worst enemy.

She saw herself with such a skewed gaze she probably had no idea what that garb did to a red-blooded male. As he only had one good eye he took another look to check his wicked imagination wasn't running riot. No, it wasn't that good, he decided, and any minute he would forget he had met her only last night and throw himself at her feet and beg if he kept eyeing the long and lovely line of her slender hips and legs like a randy youth. 'Do you really not know of the disasters you are inviting by going about dressed in breeches like that?' he asked hoarsely.

'It's practical. I used to go for long walks at night when I lived with my grandparents and everyone thought I was safely tucked up in bed. It's so much easier to move quietly without the skirts and petticoats that usually hold us females back.'

'Practical and quiet be damned,' he snapped, driven to the end of his tether by her certainty he would always behave like a gentleman whatever she did to tempt him. He hadn't done so last night and he didn't want to now.

Now she was looking shocked and he was so frustrated by her assumption it was perfectly all right to walk about with shapely, feminine legs on show in snugly fitting riding breeches. He wanted her to know it wasn't; it was temptation piled on temptation, and he was only human. And he never felt more so as he longed to strip those damned things off her and plunge into her like a satyr.

'I'm not a eunuch, Lady Melissa,' he told her harshly and saw her recoil a few steps. He felt ashamed of himself for not being the perfect gentleman who would loosen his cravat and hum and haw and pretend she was nothing out of the common way, and he should never have lit that fire and wasn't it hot in here?

'I realised that last night,' she told him coolly.

His temper tugged even harder at its tethers, but somehow he managed to clamp a firm hold on his wilder male urges and turn back to his fire making as silence stretched between them. Memory of that kiss and his endless sensual tension ever since he had set eyes on her filled it for him. Why had he insisted on putting himself through this torture of wanting and not having all over again? Wasn't one sleepless night longing for her wild and responsive in his bed enough to send him half mad without the help of those damned breeches to get him the rest of the way there?

'I think that fine blaze will do, my lord,' she told him rather gently, as if she was pacifying a bad-tempered animal. 'You wouldn't want to burn your splendid house down.'

'No,' he said, rising to his feet and wishing he didn't have to stagger a little on his weakened knee in front of her. It was a timely reminder he was not some fine matrimonial prize if he lost control of this ridiculous passion she roused in him at first glance and tried to rouse her just as fiercely back.

Hardly likely, Lathbury, he told himself as blood flowed painfully back into that knee, and he dared not move unless he tumbled over. *Why the devil would the likes of her ever want the likes of you?*

'The last thing I need is a fire burning out of control,' he said carefully.

'Quite,' she said and shot him a wary look.

He hoped his crass comment made her think harder about wearing those damned breeches on her next nocturnal adventure. If there was a next one, he would still have to go with her even if it was torture of the most refined kind. The thought of her wandering into another man's library inviting trouble made

him desperate to be there to stop her doing it, even if
it cost him his sanity.

'I will have all the books I bought at the auction
boxed up and delivered to Wiston House in the morning,' he said curtly because he had just had enough
of playing ogre tonight.

'Oh,' she said, as if she was astonished he could be
an honourable man, and it felt like a slap in the face.
'Thank you, Lathbury, you are very kind.'

'Kind?' he said disgustedly. 'Call it so if you really must, but none of it was Granger's to sell, so of
course I cannot keep them.'

'I will pay you the auction price.'

'That you will not,' he growled. 'If your blockhead
cousin chooses to pay me he can, since he sold goods
he had no right to, but I won't take your money.'

'You would if I was a man,' she said in a tight, offended voice and glared defiance at him from those
lioness eyes he wanted to gaze into until he forgot he
was hideous and she was a lady, and why couldn't she
just let him be right for once?

'No,' he said dourly. 'It is a simple matter of right
and wrong.' Although if she was a man he could return her property and let her find whatever it was on
her own and he would still be bored and sitting here
night after night, missing something richer and more
exciting he had not even known he didn't have in his
life until he met her.

'What of my grandmother's papers?' she asked
warily.

A good question and it led him on to why on earth

he hadn't had the whole lot sent to Wiston House this afternoon as a true gentleman should. Because he was desperate to see her again—not quite this much of her because he wasn't a martyr, but that was why doing the honourable thing and returning her property hadn't even occurred to him until now. And what the hell was wrong with him in that case? Anyone would think mirrors had never been invented and Lord Lathbury hadn't left his gilded youth behind when he impaled himself on a hedge and killed his best friend.

'I locked them in my desk drawer last night. They were so important to you it seemed wrong to leave them lying about. They are in the bottom drawer on the right; here's the key,' he said.

'Thank you,' she said politely as he dropped it on to her outstretched palm because he might burst into flames if he felt the touch of her soft skin against his fingertips again right now. 'This is kind of you, my lord.'

'Is it, my lady? I wonder,' he said and made himself limp restlessly round the room while she coolly sat at his desk and unlocked the drawer. 'You might as well see if whatever you are looking for is in there,' he told her as he paused by her side, 'and as I have nowhere else I need to be tonight I might as well wait to find out.'

'Indeed,' she said with only half her attention on him now those precious papers were in front of her. 'You are a kind man.'

'Good for me,' he replied tersely and almost wished he had thought to send them around to Wiston House this morning then washed his hands of the whole shadowy business.

Except then he could have no idea what reckless starts she would try next if whatever she wanted wasn't there. The written word lost its attraction with Lady Melissa here to make life more interesting than even the most excitable Gothic novel. He waited in tense silence and knew it was wrong of him to hope what she wanted wasn't there, so he had an excuse to see her again. He frowned down at the fire but the only picture that formed was of Lady Melissa Aldercombe, so painfully alone for all these years and not even aware of how much she was missing.

He was so absorbed in finding that a tragic waste of such a vital woman's potential he was almost too late to notice the faint stir as a carriage drew up outside and subdued voices in the hall said Belle and his grandmother must have come home early for some reason. If he didn't do something to avert disaster, Melissa might have to marry him, and that was a disaster she didn't deserve.

'Leave that!' he ordered her urgently. She frowned as if trying to refocus her attention on him and the world. 'You have to hide,' he told her, and where was the last place anyone would look for a lady in his library this late at night? Ridiculous question, they wouldn't look for one at all, but if she didn't hurry up they would find her here anyway. Her gaze shot to the hidden doorway and even now he couldn't abide the thought of her slipping into the night dressed like that. 'No, I'm not the only one who uses that door to slip in and out at night.'

'Where, then?' she argued as if this was his fault, and it probably was.

'In here—be sure not to make a sound,' he told her as he all but pushed her into the anteroom used by the librarian he employed a couple of days a week to tend his books.

'I thought I might sing,' she said sarcastically. The temptation to swat her neat behind so blatantly on show was nigh irresistible, but they had no time for a blazing argument. For his grandmother and sister to be home so early meant something was wrong and Belle would come and tell him what happened before she went to bed.

'Just sit still and be quiet,' he told Melissa, 'unless you prefer to marry me.'

'Never!' she told him as if she could imagine nothing worse and scuttled into the little room, shutting the door behind her.

'And don't try to light a candle,' he opened the door to tell her. The mellow light slanting into the dark room showed him my lady in such a fury she stuck her tongue out before he shut it. He wanted to march back in there and kiss her breathless so much he had to fight his baser self not to and to the devil with consequences. The thought of his little sister's face if she caught him kissing a strange woman dressed in breeches at nearly midnight sobered him so swiftly he was across the room and behind his desk when Belle opened the outer door.

'Ah, so you *are* still up.'

'Come in and tell me all about it,' he said, and Lady Melissa would just have to sit in the dark and stew or go to sleep like the weary aristocrat she should be after the alarms and excitements of the last day.

'We were tired after last night and the Flatleys' party was proving, well, flat.'

'And...'

'Why must there always be an "and", Adam? Maybe I just want to wish you goodnight.'

'You did that before you went off for the evening in high spirits. Are you going to tell me what has happened to damp them down?'

Chapter Ten

Trapped in the dark with only an uncomfortable stool to perch on, Melissa decided she might as well add furtive listening to her sins since there was nothing else to do. Adam and his sister were too far away to hear much of their murmured conversation, so she peered through the keyhole at them. Maybe he had sat on that particular sofa to keep an eye on this door and make sure she didn't risk sneaking out if his back was turned. Or maybe it was just chance he was in her line of vision.

At least she could see him and his sister as Miss Lathbury confided in her big brother, and it was touching to see how close they were, despite the gap in age. To stop herself feeling wistful about never having a sympathetic brother to confide in, Melissa did her best to watch them like a dispassionate outsider. She would have known the girl was Adam's sister even if they had met by chance despite the girl's more delicate features and her brother's very masculine ones.

Miss Lathbury was a beauty, but Melissa was far too fascinated by her brother to take much more note of the girl than that. He was sitting with the uninjured side of his face to her keyhole and *Oh, my word, but he was a handsome devil once upon a time.*

Yet it was his character that fascinated her now. The mature but tempered power of him made her knees go weak although she was kneeling on them and needed them to stay strong. The idiot thought himself such a shadow of a man and hid himself in libraries so he didn't upset nervous females. *Stupid man*, she decided with a worryingly indulgent smile. Didn't he know he was far more fascinating now than if he had kept the Adonis-like perfection and shining self-confidence of a handsome young lord with every advantage of birth and fortune?

Obviously not, and perhaps it was just as well for discerning ladies like her. He would take the fiery attraction between them no further because he thought he was repulsive, and she had to be glad, even when he was so wrong about himself it hurt her. She shifted as her knees threatened not to hold her in this cramped position much longer. Flexing her toes, she almost groaned as the blood flowed back, and the discomfort was a distraction from watching Lord Lathbury talk to his little sister with such fascinated eyes.

'There you are. I thought you must have sneaked in here while I was busy telling Scrooby to make up a tisane for you. I would have thought you had caused enough trouble for one evening without dragging your brother into it, miss,' a much louder voice than his or Miss Lathbury's interrupted them.

Melissa was very glad there was a door and this darkness between her and Adam's grandmother. She still smiled at the sound of Her Ladyship scolding them even as she fussed over her granddaughter like a mother hen. The thought of what the forthright Dowager would say if she found Melissa in the dark straining to hear every word should make her clap her hands over her ears and pretend she was a hundred miles away, but it didn't.

'And what rigmarole are you reading now?' she heard the Dowager Lady Lathbury demand brusquely.

Melissa risked getting cramp again to peer from her keyhole in frustration, but she could only see Adam. Somehow she knew the effort it cost him to sit there looking mildly amused while his grandparent peered at the papers Melissa was sorting through when they were interrupted. All of a sudden she was desperately hoping one of the letters she wrote to her own grandmother pleading to keep her baby wasn't there.

'I was going through the papers I bought with Mrs Granger's books,' he said casually. He didn't even turn his head to watch his grandmother and Melissa had to admire his coolness as her own heartbeat seemed so loud she was surprised they didn't hear it.

'Now she was a woman after my own heart,' his grandmother said, and it warmed Melissa's to hear such a strong woman say so even if she did wish the

Dowager Lady Lathbury would stop being curious and go away. 'Had a fine mind and some sound ideas about educating females. More facts and ideas and less fancy and flummery would put a stop to all this posturing and flapping about over nothing modern women think clever. Now in my day…'

'Spare us your favourite homily on the degenerate times we live in,' Adam teased.

'Rude boy.'

'Yes, but it's late, and if you are going to Lady Carroway's Venetian breakfast tomorrow, you will need your beauty sleep. Although why it is called breakfast when it takes place in the afternoon and is nothing like any breakfast I ever ate is beyond me.'

'We had picnics in my day, plain and simple.'

'Back in Shangri-La again, are we, darling?' he said with a smile that warmed Melissa through to her toes, although, come to think of it, she was beginning to lose all feeling in them again so she needed all the warmth she could get.

'We had more *fun* than you young things seem to,' the lady said with a sigh.

'I have quite enough excitement in my life, thank you.'

'Hah! How can you call it fun sitting here night after night, living in your head instead of enjoying real life? You need to get out more, my lad.'

'Rooms full of people chattering like magpies might be your idea of a splendid night's entertainment, but it isn't mine,' he said lightly.

'You used to enjoy it.'

'I used to be a mindless young fribble hell-bent on my own selfish pleasures. Now I am a sober and middle-aged gentleman I prefer my library of an evening. You might be surprised at the unexpected delights I find in here when you are busy elsewhere.'

'Never mind plaguing poor Adam about his scholarly ways again, Grandmama. We should have gone straight to bed and left him in peace,' Miss Lathbury said, and Melissa guessed she was doing her best to divert the lady from a sore subject.

'Little wonder you are tired after that fuss and to-do last night, Belle. An earlier night than you expected will do you good, even if it would be stretching things to call it an early one,' Adam said.

'Yes, and that tisane you are going to make me drink will be going cold by now, Grandmama.'

'I can't think why you didn't go straight up after insisting you were too weary to go on to the Patmore ball tonight,' the lady replied tartly.

'I am,' Miss Lathbury said and managed to sound it this time.

They lingered for a few more moments and Melissa decided it was very silly to be jealous Adam was probably kissing them goodnight and wishing them sweet dreams. It was only because she missed her own grandmother that she was wistful about him bidding goodnight to his family.

Melissa shook her head at her own stupidity and pictured a very different version of herself at the centre of Adam Lathbury's world, being kissed breathless as they slowly followed the rest of the family upstairs to the lovely privacy of the master suite. Of course, the imaginary Lady Melissa Lathbury would never have loved any other man but this one, never have put herself beyond the pale as a nobleman's wife by bearing another man's child out of wedlock. The charmed creature she might have been, if she had fallen in love with the dashing Baron Lathbury at first sight all those years ago and he with her, did look like a very fortunate woman from here, though. By now they would have been married for several years and have a promising tribe of children to dote on, worry about and delight in.

Of course, the terror of Adam's accident and all the desperate weeks and months of hoping and praying for his recovery would have been almost too much to bear for a loving wife, but it would have been worth it to love him with her whole heart and soul. She still shuddered in her dark corner of his fine library at the thought he might have died from his injuries without this Melissa even knowing how important he could have been to her if things were different.

Best forget that fanciful version of herself as his beloved and loving wife so she would not slump into a corner and weep for what might have been—if only their stars had aligned and he had been in the least bit interested in headstrong Lady Melissa Aldercombe when she came out nearly a decade ago, as she would have if she hadn't been so busy grieving for another man and the child she had to give away before she was even old enough to make her debut in the polite world.

'Much as I love them, I do sometimes wish they

were a hundred miles away,' the real Adam Lathbury informed her gruffly when he opened the door to her prison-cum-sanctuary.

She hadn't even realised the others were gone and it was safe to come out. She was still on her knees after staring sightlessly at the empty chaise and dreaming of impossible things. She blinked and even soft candlelight hurt her eyes after so long in the dark. 'Help me up,' she demanded, praying he would not see she had shed tears for the lives they could have led but didn't.

'Yes, milady, anything you say, milady,' he said with a mocking grin.

'You are very annoying, Lord Lathbury.'

'Adam.'

'Thank you, Adam,' she said rather ungraciously as he tugged her to her feet. She wobbled as blood rushed back into them. 'I am very stiff.'

'You would be, after spending so long on your knees.'

She staggered over to the sofa he had sat on with his sister while she recovered. 'Would you rather I rolled into a dark corner and worked myself into hysterics?'

'No,' he said on a long sigh as he sat down beside her as if all the strength had gone out of his knees as well. 'I would rather you were back at Wiston House and safely asleep in your own bed,' he told her and pushed his fingers through his hair as if he really meant it.

Hurt threatened while her sensible side argued he

was right. Yet even so her fingers itched to comb his now wildly curling dark pelt into something like order again and feel the crisp vitality of it and maybe ruffle it up again for the sheer pleasure of being so close to him. It would be such a giveaway and tenderly rueful gesture that she shook her head and sat on her hands to stop them doing it.

'Safety is overrated,' she argued and realised it was true. Better to be with him and in danger of whatever she was in danger of than sleeping the night away and waking up to a life as smooth and safe as she had thought she wanted it to be for so long.

'Not when this stupid idea could have led to disaster it isn't,' he told her, and she felt him tense at her side as if he was about to get up and pace again.

'Don't,' she said, putting out a hand to stop him before he got to his feet. 'You will wear out your beautiful carpet,' she added when she remembered she had no right to say what he should and should not do.

He said something very rude about his carpet, but relaxed into his seat again and sighed as if the cares of the world were on his shoulders. It was no good; she had to turn her head to watch him and he looked so weary and tense she reached her hand towards him and snatched it back when tension seemed to jar through him.

'Don't you know I'm the worst danger you could meet?' he ground out as if she was being obtuse and reckless with that almost touch. 'The brutal truth is I want you, my lady. I wanted you from the moment I saw you last night, before you looked up and saw me standing there and staring back at you like a starving beast. I want you any way I can have you, but on your back frantically begging for everything a man and woman can give each other in the wildest extremes of passion is my favourite. No, make that need, not want, and see sense about this mission you are so set on carrying off alone.

'You must accept my help, but at least you will know what you are risking if you refuse to. You are nigh irresistible temptation for any red-blooded male you happen to stumble across in your headlong pursuit of whatever you are looking for. I have just enough strength of will left to ignore my needs and wants and remember you are a lady, even if you seldom remember it yourself.'

'I have to keep looking,' she said, carefully ignoring the exasperation in his deep voice because if he really did want her it was best not to leap into his arms and risk any balance he had found in his life after it shattered. Having him over her, inside her, driving her to new extremes of passion as they climbed to the ultimate fulfilment together might allay the hot demand and shocking need she had been fighting so hard since she looked up and saw him standing there, so intent on her it felt as if he was burnt into her very soul as she fought for air and coolness and normality to counter the threat he posed *her* hard-won serenity. 'You should leave me to carry on with my quest alone, Adam. The likes of you should not tangle with the likes of me.'

It was as close to a warning as she dared give him

she was noxious, but of course he took it the wrong way. She saw that from the storm of emotion in his good eye that had gone so dark with fury and frustration the velvet brown iris was lost in black temper. He thought she meant he wasn't good enough for her rather than the other way about and looked every inch the stern fighting baron his ancestors must have been in their full power.

How could he think so much less of himself because of a few scars and some old injuries? But he was right to warn her about the risk. She was out of her depth with such a potent and masculine man. Her Joe was still a boy when they had last made love; of course he was a boy turning into the strong, big-hearted man he would have been if he lived long enough, but he hadn't. She would never forget him, but Adam, Lord Lathbury, was here, right now and next to her, and he urgently desired her; this very adult and powerful male wanted to be her lover and how dearly she wanted to oblige him. Nothing could reason it away and goodness she had tried to.

She knew he said that to frighten her, but her inner rebel wanted him so ravenously it yearned to be under, over, together and with him in the ultimate act of love every bit as much as he said he wanted her there, like that. The wild girl who had taken the ultimate risk for love all those years ago was alive again, eager to be reminded how it felt to want with every fibre of her being and not regret a word or move of grabbing it with both hands.

That reckless little idiot could almost feel the hot

glory inside her at the very thought of it flame into an inferno as they got these breeches off her at long last and made much better use of this chaise to sate this glorious passion he had hurled at her like a weapon. She wanted to throw his words back at him until fire ran heady and strong through them both and he could not resist the power of it. It was like trying to hold back a force of nature inside as the twist of heat and almost pain of strong need wound into a demand for the ultimate satisfaction that was so very hard to ignore it actually hurt her to clamp chains on it.

'Impossible for a duke's daughter to want an apology of a baron,' he said flatly, and she had to push aside a fog of overheated desire and frustration to recall her reply to his driven declaration he wanted her. She shook her head so frantically her unruly hair began to tumble out of its harsh pins and she impatiently ignored it.

'No! That's not what I meant at all,' she argued hotly. She was unworthy of him, not the other way about. How reckless of her to even hint at the truth, but it didn't matter because he had turned her words on their heads and stabbed himself on them instead.

'If you say so,' he said as if so convinced he was right there was no point arguing.

'I do say so,' she persisted anyway.

He looked as if he didn't even want to believe her, then he turned away as if his limp and scars and her lofty birth were the only reason he could think of for her to refuse to talk about her quest. She shook her head to deny it to his broad and now hunched back, as if the bleakness of her imagined rejection had brought his old hurts back to life. It was letting him fight a familiar enemy instead of the false version of her he was so busily making up in his head so he could ignore the real one, and maybe she ought to let him do just that.

'I…' she began to say and goodness knew what she might have said if he gave her a chance.

'Will you promise to tell me if you find what you are looking for if I send everything I have from Mrs Granger's collection to Wiston House tomorrow?' he demanded as he suddenly swung round to confront her again. He either hadn't heard her start to speak or didn't want to hear what she had to say. She should harden her fast-beating heart and let him think the worst of her.

'Very well,' she said. It would be much easier than having him about to distract her while she went through Grandmother Granger's papers.

'Then I shall have them sent to Wiston House in the morning with the books.'

'You will?'

'I will,' he said in a tight, hard voice and strode over to his desk and shuffled her grandmother's papers together and stuffed them back in the drawer before locking it again while she was still trying to think of something to say.

'Thank you,' she said at last.

'My pleasure,' he lied savagely. 'Now we need to get you home before we get caught together in the middle of the night and you have to marry me anyway.'

'You're coming with me?' she said clumsily.

'No, I thought I'd leave you to the mercy of the human wolves that prowl the night even in tamed Mayfair, Lady Melissa,' he told her with such biting irony she winced.

'I doubt you'd do that to your worst enemy,' she argued stiffly.

'But you don't know me, do you?' he said, and who would have thought it could hurt so much to be made back into the strangers they should have been all along?

'Evidently not,' she replied, although she wanted to argue so passionately she had to clamp her teeth to keep the words in. It was best he thought the worst of her—best for him, anyway—and silence lay heavy and tense between them for a few long seconds.

'Come on then,' he said impatiently and marched to the hidden door as if he knew she would follow like an obedient dog.

She did, after weighing up the idea of staying where she was or dealing with this wild see-saw of emotions in the peace and quiet of her own bedroom and deciding on the latter. She was tired of fighting a force of nature, tired of remembering exactly why she must keep on doing it. One moment she was lost in the peace of his beloved library last night; the next there he was. He was the fire and hurt and promise she refused to dream about until she looked up, stepped outside time and met his gaze, promise for reckless promise. In this time and this life they were promises she could not keep because of vows she had made to another man, even if they never got as far as making them in front of a priest.

Now here she was with Lord Lathbury, the man she wanted and couldn't have. They were already outside the house and somehow she couldn't catch her breath and be glad. Their brief and eventful acquaintance was nearly over so she was glad of a few seconds' respite while he locked the door behind him. It felt pathetic to linger over every last second of being with him because never seeing him again felt so stark and lonely.

This time the night felt cold and dark as he pocketed the key and still said nothing, as if eager to be done with her. Every step of their walk to Wiston House took a second off their last pinch of time together, but they crept silently through the byways between his house and her father's and she rejected all the words she badly wanted to say to him, but could not.

I want you right back, my lord, but you will not want to marry me after we have taken our pleasure of one another and I confess what I once did for love.

She could not give Joe and her son's secrets up, or risk another illegitimate child being born of her hot and hasty passion for a mature man instead of a young lover. It would break her if she had to part with another baby so it could have a decent life away from its scandalous mother. Even so, she had to fight an urgent need to pull this man back and kiss him in a dark alley where they could take their pleasure of one another with no questions asked.

The idea was so wickedly heady she clamped her hands into fists at her side to stop them reaching for him and to hell with the consequences. He would be so hurt if she let her inner she-wolf out and led them headlong into disaster. Even so her nails bit into her palms and her breath felt tight in her chest when he halted warily. It seemed too soon for them to be outside Wiston House already, but they still were, and now he would soon be gone from her life for good. Somehow she could not bring herself to say goodbye knowing he would always think of her as a heartless snob, if he thought of her at all.

'You are a very fine baron, my lord,' she argued with his bitter assertion she didn't think he was good enough.

'And you are a duke's daughter.'

'For all the good it does me,' she mumbled bitterly, and she should be glad; temptation was so much easier to resist when only one of them was struggling against it.

'For all the good you *let* it do you,' he argued softly.

'Maybe I am as stubborn as you. You think you're less because of a few scars and a limp that doesn't even slow you down.'

'What's your excuse, then?'

She drew breath to tell him and slowly let it out again, because of course she couldn't. 'I don't have one,' she lied and almost felt his disappointment.

'We're back to lords and ladies then,' he said and reached past her to open the garden door. 'Goodnight,

Lady Melissa,' he said coldly and all but pushed her through it.

The moon came out from behind the clouds and made his face a mix of silver light and brooding shadows. 'Goodnight, Adam,' she whispered.

With a last look at her staring at him from her side of the moonlit garden he bowed his head in some sort of salute or goodbye and walked away. She watched him leave as if he could hardly wait to forget he had ever met her, and it was like bidding goodbye to a dream she should never have let herself have. She softly closed the garden door and crept across the garden and sought her lonely bed. Of course she wasn't going to cry herself to sleep over a man she hardly knew.

Chapter Eleven

Apparently two nights of stealthy adventures and too much stormy emotion were not enough to make her sleep properly. Melissa woke up after a harsh dream and tried to go on with her morning as if there was nothing wrong, but she was lying. She had lost Adam's good opinion and his company and the wonderful feeling she was not alone with her problems any more. It was nonsensical to mourn something she never truly had, but she still felt forlorn and lonely.

She busied herself sorting out the China Room, making lists of what was missing and must be replaced after her father's long years without a hostess. If she could make him comfortable again, maybe she could patch up some sort of life here as a politician's daughter; if she could find that letter *and* forget Adam Lathbury——what a challenge that was going to be.

She sighed and tried to concentrate on dinner plates, but her thoughts kept drifting back to him and she lost count yet again. He had such ridiculous ideas about his scars and a slight limp and he could be totally exasperating. He didn't smile very often either, but when he did it warmed her to her very toes and lots of places in between she had promised herself she would not think about.

Then there was the deep rumble of his laugh when he forgot those supposed flaws and became the man Nature intended him to be. Oh, drat the man; she was lost in thought again and this list was never going to get made if she didn't snap out of this stupid abstraction and get on with real life.

'Ah, here you are, my lady. The Duke wishes to speak with you.'

'Thank you, Carnforth, is my father in his study?'

'No, my lady, in the library,' the butler said.

'Tell His Grace I will join him there as soon as I have washed my hands, and please don't wait for me. There is no need to announce me to my own father.'

'Very well, my lady,' the man said gloomily and went away again.

After a hasty wash and remembering to remove the apron her father would raise his eyebrows at, Melissa ran downstairs, trying to look bright and cheerful so he would not worry about her any more than he did already. So she breezed into the room. 'Yes, Papa? What is it?' she said and stopped in her tracks.

She stared at three large crates and Adam Lathbury standing by them looking dashing and much too composed. Her heartbeat thundered with shock at the sight of him in her home and looking so coolly calm, but luckily her father spoke up before she could give her panic or this secret delight away.

'You will be delighted to hear Lord Lathbury is set on returning your grandmother's books and papers, my dear. You never told me you tripped and would have fallen if Lathbury here had not saved you from coming a cropper when you went for that walk in the Park yesterday morning. You must have been very shaken to tell him about your disappointment at your lost legacy, but I dare say you had no idea he had purchased some of it. Lathbury has decided it is only right to return them to you and I am sure you are very grateful.'

'Good morning, my lord, and thank you very much. This is so kind of you,' she said as effusively as she could manage with her father's speculative gaze on them and the shock of Adam's presence here in broad daylight still sinking in.

'Good morning, Lady Melissa,' Adam said with a graceful bow and a bland smile.

Melissa gave the boxes a stern look. She should be grateful and gracious, but Adam coming here was a direct challenge. He knew it wasn't what she wanted and she could tell from his faintly mocking air as he met her accusing look that he was forcing their relationship on to another level when she had thought it was all but over.

Ten minutes ago she had been missing him so much it hurt. Now he was here she didn't know how she felt any more. There was so much she wanted to say to him and so little she could say with her father looking so delighted she had taken a first step to becoming part of the *haut ton* by stumbling over a strange man in the Park.

'I am very grateful for your kindness, my lord. But I did not tell you that sad tale expecting such generosity. I should never have told you why I was in a brown study when I nearly fell headlong yesterday,' she said.

'It would be wrong of me to keep something your cousin had no right to sell, Lady Melissa,' the wretch said and raised an eyebrow as if almost insulted she thought he might.

'I should still not have told you the cause of my reverie, Lord Lathbury,' she told him with a hot look behind her father's back to say *stop*.

'Yet I am glad you did, my lady,' Adam said with a sad shake of his dark head and a challenge in his good eye to say he wasn't as easy to dismiss as she thought. Her inner wanton was hopping and skipping because Adam was back in her life. *She* was delighted to yearn for him like a besotted fool again while the rest of her wished he had stayed away.

Adam blandly met Melissa's stormy gaze and tried to pretend he was a gentleman. All he wanted right now was to be his old self again so he could throw her over his shoulder, summon his fiery steed and carry her off to his castle until she was his in every way a woman could be besotted and entangled with her passionate and very eager lover. Once she had agreed never to keep secrets from him again and trust him to keep the wolves at bay for the rest of their fairy tale, they could settle into driving one another crazy for the rest of their lives.

Hmm, perhaps they would detour to Lathbury House first and lock out the rest of the world while they slaked this fierce passion first. It would ruin the romance if they had to stop at several deserted spots along the way to drive one another witless with mutual desire and blissful fulfilment. And too much of him was threatening not to be gentlemanly at all at the very thought of something that was never going to happen. Even if he could be a dashing young blade again, he doubted she would passively agree to forget the rest of the world for his sake.

So, he didn't come here for any of that then, did he? No, he came because he had sensed her slipping away from him last night and walling herself back into lonely isolation. He'd left her standing in the moonlight watching him warily, as if she knew she had brushed with something dangerous and was determined to avoid it from now on. Somehow he had managed not to turn back to kiss her until they both knew she was right: he was dangerous.

Instead he went home and paced his empty-feeling master bedchamber as he was in no mood to sit in a library that reminded him too acutely of her and everything he wanted to be to her and with her. She had responded hungrily to his kiss the first night, seemed to feel the bite of fiery attraction he had to believe was mutual if he was to stay sane, but she so badly didn't want to want him.

He sensed a huge hurt had once happened to her more than ever as they spent more time together. It felt as if she had once taken a wild risk that had failed and left her so lonely and bereft she would never willingly take another. She needed the life and light she had denied herself for so long and he intended her to get it. He was determined to pull her out of the shadows, even if he would step back when she was in the land of the living again, because she deserved the best after spending so long alone and lonely, and he certainly wasn't that.

'If only I had thought before I spoke,' she said as lightly as if they had only met once and in public, 'and I should have looked where I was going and not allowed my tongue to run on wheels.'

'Not at all, my lady, these things are rightfully yours. I am surprised your legal advisers have not been in touch with me to correct their mistake.'

'There, you see, Melissa, I said we should let the lawyers deal with it,' her father said blandly, and of course the Duke would try to convince an outsider it was a trifling matter.

Except Adam already knew this was important so the Duke was wasting his breath. So, Melissa did not confide fully in her own father. Adam was more certain than ever that she needed to be prised out of her stern solitude before she wasted all her youth and beauty and uniqueness on regretting whatever it was she had to regret.

'No need to involve them, Your Grace, and I hope

you will accept the return of your property without a tiresome argument, Lady Melissa. I shall discuss this matter with the other buyers my secretary noted down at the sale. I can appeal to their gentlemanly instincts on your behalf since you cannot do so yourself as a single lady.' Adam met her gaze with a challenge in his not to argue. If she thought her glare back was going to make him give up and go away like a good little lord, she was doomed to disappointment.

'Lathbury *can* openly ask for them as you cannot, my dear,' her father said as if it was regrettable, but there was no point in fighting reality.

Melissa bit her lip and gave in, for now. 'Then I must thank you for your efforts on my behalf, Lord Lathbury,' she said meekly, but if he really thought she would let him fight her battles for her he was deluded.

'I hope you succeed, Lathbury,' her father said with a wry smile as if this was merely an annoying trifle. 'Granger is a fool and your actions show him in a poor light.'

'Lady Melissa seems to think Mrs Granger's scholarship was an embarrassment to her grandson,' Adam said just as smoothly, but would Papa believe she had told him so after a single casual meeting in the Park? Melissa had to hope so, because if he looked further into her dealings with Adam Lathbury her father might realise they went far deeper than one brief encounter.

'I always wondered how he managed to be such a fool with grandparents like those,' her father said, and he must be a little unnerved by this visit as well to have been so indiscreet. Did he suspect Adam knew more about his daughter than he wanted him to, then? 'But as the boy's mother is a widgeon that probably accounts for it.'

'Oh, Papa,' Melissa said and rolled her eyes as if exasperated when she was grateful to him for providing a flow of idle chatter to pass the requisite twenty minutes before a polite morning visit could be considered politely over. 'The poor woman cannot help it and my cousin Vernon probably cannot either.'

'And at least no harm has been done to this part of your inheritance, my dear. I must thank you again for these books, Lathbury. They mean a lot to my daughter.'

'It is my pleasure to return Lady Melissa's property,' Adam said, and no doubt he was telling the truth, since he seemed to be enjoying himself far too much.

She was acutely aware of his interest in the interplay between her and her father as well as their reception of him. Adam returned her sharp look with a bland social smile. This was a new side of him and should teach her not to trust his gruff and night-time self, if they were ever closeted together by night again, and there was no reason why they should be. She would be much more wary of him now she had seen the smooth and dangerous rake he once was behind the scars and the bitterness of all he had lost.

'We are embarrassing you with our repeated thanks, my lord, and I hope you will at least join us in a glass of claret to celebrate the return of all these books,' her father said with a rueful look at the crates taking up so much room in his elegant book room.

'Of course, Papa, but there's no need to ring for Carnforth,' Melissa said, glad to avoid Adam's gaze for a few moments while she poured three glasses.

'My daughter has a steadier hand than I have,' her father explained genially.

Not today, Melissa argued silently as she fought the power and temptation of Adam's attention on her every move even as he exchanged small talk with her father.

'Here you are, Papa,' she said, 'Lord Lathbury.'

'I hope you will join us, Lady Melissa,' the wretch said, raising an eyebrow at the third glass she had left on the side table because she needed every drop of self-control she could muster with him here to test her temper to the limits with his smooth beau-about-town act, or was her pirate the act and this cynical man of the world the real Adam Lathbury?

'Of course,' she said colourlessly. She sipped at her glass and shot him a hostile glare behind her father's back to tell him to stop baiting her and go away.

'And it is always my pleasure to do a lady a service,' Lathbury said piously.

I bet it is, she thought darkly.

'You are very kind, my lord,' she told him out loud. There was a noise outside and her father seemed distracted, although Melissa wasn't sure he didn't have eyes in the back of his head after his years on the government benches.

'I am so glad you think so, Lady Melissa,' Adam replied smoothly.

Liar, she mouthed at him when her father turned away to listen a little harder to who was out there and frowned as if he was faced with a dilemma—duty to his daughter or his country, she could almost hear him debating with himself.

'That sounds like Marshmain,' the Duke said at last. 'I know you will not keep my daughter past the correct time, Lathbury,' he added with a frown.

'Of course he will not, Papa. I know you must see what your Private Secretary requires of you this time,' Melissa told him. 'I am sure Lord Lathbury will excuse you.'

'Very well, my dear. Duty calls, I fear, Lathbury. Thank you again and good day.' With a quick bow the Duke went to see what business of state had come to a head this time.

'The Duke is a man of affairs,' Adam observed sagely as they listened to a soft exchange of greetings and a click as her father's study door closed behind them.

'Indeed,' she said repressively.

'He is highly thought of by other men of affairs,' he added with a mocking grin to tell her he wasn't going away so she might as well talk to him.

'Yes,' she replied curtly.

'Cat got your tongue, Lady Melissa?' he murmured.

'No, I am always like this when I am forced into company against my will,' she told him, and had no idea why she thought she was going to miss him so dreadfully before he had turned up bold as brass. Was he keeping her off balance by being unpredictable? And, if so, what was he intending to achieve by it?

'I thought you might like to thank me properly for doing as I promised,' he said as if last night's prickly conversation never happened.

'Thank you, my lord.'

'Adam,' he corrected very softly, and how had he got so close without all her senses screaming a warning?

'Thank you, Adam. Why are you really here?'

'Just fulfilling a promise,' he said, and the teasing look leeched out of his visible eye and left it hard to meet, but she was a woman of character so she did so anyway.

'And reminding me of mine,' she said.

'Yes, I felt that I needed to,' he said with another dour look.

He was right, of course. She had been thinking of sending word she had found what she was looking for and there was no need for him to give the matter another thought.

'Very well. I will let you know if I find what I am looking for in one of them,' she said as casually as she could, and she knew if the letter wasn't here he would feel obliged to help her search the other collectors' lots. It should not feel such a relief or maybe even the perfect excuse to spend more time with him, but it still did.

'And if not we will just have to keep looking,' he said cheerfully enough. Maybe she was only a diversion from being forced out of his own isolation to watch over his little sister this Season, but she hated the thought of him squirming under the half-horrified, half-fascinated gaze of the *ton*. Somehow she hated the repellent idea he might have kissed her as a welcome change from doing his duty by his family even more.

So she said, 'The search goes on only for me', and she would rather do it alone than hear this sneering voice in her head say *He's only with you because he doesn't want to be out in the polite world.*

'Like Ruth among the alien corn, "whither thou goest, I will go"—or at least as far as your nocturnal adventures in other men's libraries are concerned I will,' he argued easily enough, as if once he said so then so it would be.

'I am nothing to you,' she said starkly. This sense of being vulnerable and exposed was his fault. Before she had met him she had dreaded discovery for her son's sake and now she hated the very thought of it on her own account as well, and confound the man for making her care that much what the world thought of her.

'I don't think you know what you are, my lady. You have never had enough of a taste of the real world to find out.'

She suppressed a moan at the reminder of that

sense—it wanted the taste of him on her tongue nearly as badly as her skin wanted the touch of him everywhere a man could get. 'You don't know anything about me,' she managed to say as if that was all she was thinking about. She censored the rest of her wild thoughts and tried to lock desire away until his sharp, intelligent gaze wasn't on her and she could reason it to powder.

'Then tell me,' he challenged, and she clenched her fists at her sides and turned to stare out of the long windows at the fine garden of her father's house in its full spring daytime glory and managed to resist a foolish temptation to do just that.

'No,' she said with her back to him.

'Very well, I'll wait until you trust me enough and ask again.'

'I never will.'

'We shall see. For now I really must go; I am a busy man,' he told her as if they had been discussing the weather and he had a more important appointment to hurry off to.

'Then I bid you a good day, my lord.'

'Good day, Melissa,' he said from far too close behind her again. For a big man, with that limp he was supposed to be so conscious of, he could move with remarkable stealth and agility when he wanted to.

She felt his breath warm her exposed neck, and awareness flamed down her backbone like wildfire until it shot tingles to the very tips of her toes and fingers. She held herself as still as a statue and willed her racing heart and pent-up breath to calm and not give away how desperate she was for his touch.

'Try to miss me,' he whispered against the vulnerable knot of nerves at the nape of her neck. Why did she ask for her hair to be arranged in a simple knot high on her head today and make it this easy for him to tease the sensual charge between them back into a primal force of nature?

Oh, I will, she refused to whisper out loud. The power of speech and even rational thought left her anyway as he pressed a brief kiss to the sensitised skin he had already teased into sensory awareness by not quite touching it. Even with that warning she was surprised by the sheer raw need that swept through her at just a fleeting kiss. Her eyes widened as she searched the glass in front of her for his reflection and was frustrated that there was just an impression of dark hair and well-dressed lord as his kiss cooled on her vulnerable skin and she couldn't even see him properly.

Her knees wobbled and her breath came short in the quiet watchfulness of this wide and airy room, with Carnforth out there in the hall on the other side of the open door and all this breathless wanting ripping through her and driving her halfway between pleasure and pain. There could be no relief for either of them from this sweet torturous ache, yet it felt so good to be alive again that her inner wanton was crying out for all the more they could never have. If only she didn't want him so much, maybe she could be glad she had met him the other night instead of rue-

ing this deep and never-ending frustration because
Lady Melissa Aldercombe could never risk taking
another lover.

'And you can be very sure that I will miss you,
my lady,' he added huskily and gave a long sigh as if
he didn't think one brief kiss on her sensitised skin
was enough either, but this was broad daylight and
they were in her father's house and it was high time
he left, before things got even more heated than they
already were.

Then he did just that; he simply walked away with
a rueful look and a quick bow of farewell to a nodding
acquaintance. He left her clinging to the windowsill
in order to stay upright, since all her limbs had turned
to water. Hearing another murmur of male voices as
Adam exchanged a few words with the butler, she
knew it was safe to let out a stuttering sigh and lean
her forehead against the cool glass because he was
gone. She heard the door close behind him and the
house settled back to its accustomed calm.

No need to go cross-eyed in order to see her own
reflection in the windowpane because she felt the
wild heat on her cheeks, heard her soft gasps to get
enough air in her lungs to reach past what he had done
before he left her longing for more. The hurried gallop
of her heart, even as the lingering feel of his mouth
on her skin and the shake in her hand as she raised it
to her sulky unkissed mouth to try to stop it missing
him, said she should be glad he'd gone.

Instead it all gave her away as longing for so much
more—for everything, in fact. So, of course, she had

no need to see proof he had almost undone her with one touch of his mouth on her nape. Now she was longing for him with every bit of her and she couldn't have him. She had no right to want him until she could hardly recall her own name, yet she still did.

Chapter Twelve

Adam cursed softly as he walked down the steps of Wiston House. After all his noble resolutions to be Lady Melissa's Galahad, to force her to join the rest of the human race and not lock herself away like a nun any more as well, following her to that window to say a private farewell out of earshot of Wiston's butler was his latest mistake in a long line of them since he met her and wanted everything he couldn't have from a single lady of such impeccable birth and stunning looks.

Today he had watched her turn her head and try not to care if he was still there or not. It woke up all his inner devils and got him over there, standing behind her as if he still had some right to her sensual curiosity about him as a lover before his brain could stop him. Then he had kissed her like the brash, entitled fool he was before he lost his looks and his best friend. And now he was rigid with wanting her, and if he didn't change the subject every fool in London with the courage to look at him would see for themselves he was rampant and aching with it.

Fighting for enough strength of purpose to find ice and glaciers in his imagination, he limped through the back lanes and past the mews he was beginning to know so well, ignoring surprised looks from anyone unused to seeing a finely dressed gentleman storming along as if he had a dozen devils on his tail.

'I am not to be disturbed,' he informed an equally surprised footman when he strode in through the side door of his own house and slammed the concealed door to his library shut behind him.

At last he could pace in peace and be as hotly frustrated and needy as he chose. He locked the outer door in case Belle or his grandmother came to tell him something they thought he ought to know and found him too aroused to hide it. When he recalled the feel of Melissa's fine skin under his lips, the temptation of her slender neck and the tremble that went down her backbone when his mouth whispered over her nape soft as butterfly wings, he went as hard as granite.

How he had needed her, longed to seize and take and slake this endless, torturous need—with a houseful of servants and her father only a few yards away. He'd had to bolt, then stamp away to hide himself here for the shame of wanting her so urgently, like the monster in an ancient legend concealing his obsession from the gods.

'Why the devil did you leave her that note, Lathbury?' he demanded out loud as he limped up and down, cursing his last ridiculous words to her when he ought to have known he wasn't capable of being the noble knight who rescued the lady from her dragons so she could run to another man the moment she was free again.

'You're the biggest fool in Christendom and if you send another note around now to say you can't meet her after all she'll know why. She will know you're as weak as water as far as she's concerned and risk her doing everything alone for the sake of her secret rather than trust you.'

The thought of her despising him for a shilly-shallying fool felt even worse than having to turn up and pretend she was no more to him than a companion in an evening of discovery. He would suffer the torments of the damned with her at his side when he needed so much more than butterfly kisses when she trembled under them and gave that sweet little gasp for the more they must never have because it wouldn't be fair or right of him to trap her into marriage with a monster.

Meet me at the usual time, usual place.

That was what the note on top of her grandmother's sheaf of papers said, and Melissa had no idea why she was doing what he ordered. So, here she was, waiting for him in the dark with the shuffling and stir of the city night seeming so loud all around her without him here to take the edge off the hurry and danger of it all at this time of night. She shifted in her dark corner and wished she had put on her breeches and never mind what he said about them. They were warmer and a lot less restricting than this narrow-skirted dark gown would be if she was forced to run for her life.

She shivered and fitted herself even more closely into the low doorway that the gardeners used to take things in and out without troubling anyone else. Thank goodness her cloak was warm and dark so she could blend in as long as she kept still and hoped nobody was sharp enough to pick her from the gloom.

'Ah, there you are,' Adam's deep voice murmured out of the night and sounded as if she was the one who was late and he had been standing here for an age instead of her.

'You're late,' she grumbled.

'And you have missed me?'

How did he know that? *Because you are standing here waiting for him like a besotted idiot*, she told herself severely and stood up straighter.

'Here,' he said and passed her a mask and what felt like a domino.

'What am I supposed to do with them?'

'Wear them, of course.'

'Why?'

'Because you will look conspicuous at a masquerade if you don't,' he said and went striding off into the night before she caught her breath to demand more information.

'Why would I want to go to one of those?' she managed to say a little breathlessly as she caught up with the exasperating man like a dinghy rowed after a galleon.

'Hush, we can argue when we are away from here, or would you like to be caught here with me by the Duke or his neighbours?'

For someone who wanted to be quiet he seemed to have a lot to say. She sniffed rather loudly to let him know what she thought of his arrogance, but still did as he said and held her tongue until they were in a broader street. She marvelled at his certainty about where they were going in this dangerous city with its patchwork of lights and shadows, relatively safe and unsafe. She felt like a country mouse as she took his silently offered arm and clung on to his warmth for dear life.

'*Now* can I ask what on earth you think you're doing?' she asked him at last.

'Showing you some of the real world we talked about last time we met,' he said, and she had to cast her mind back and come up with his assertion that she hadn't seen enough of the world to know who she really was.

'I don't want to taste any more life than I already have,' she told him crossly and would have snatched her hand away from his crooked elbow except he had sneakily extended his arm until they were hand in hand instead of arm in arm. It felt so intimate and safe there she left it where it was. No point being a fool for the sake of her pride when who knew what might happen if she didn't stay close to him in the suddenly teeming streets.

'How do you know if you haven't tried it?' he asked.

'I just do,' she said absently, fascinated by the bustle and noise and the bewildering mixture of people who were strolling around at this time of night as if it was broad daylight. Thank goodness for the mask and domino, she decided, as fops and poorer youths ogled her as if she was fair game, and she clung to Adam's hand and was relieved when they took one look at his powerful shoulders and backed off. 'And I don't have an invitation,' she protested.

'You don't usually let that stop you,' he replied, and she could tell that he was smiling from the sound of his voice. The fact she could read his moods from the way he spoke felt worryingly intimate, but at least the shadows between brightly lit shops and street lamps hid her expression even from him, and she was wearing a mask so she could dream openly and he wouldn't even know she was eyeing him like an adoring lover as the noise and smells of the nighttime streets faded into the background. So what was the point of him showing her more of their capital city when she was more fascinated by him than the abundant life around them?

'I don't need to find anything wherever you are taking me, unless one of your fellow scholars is holding a masquerade ball, and my father would have found out and told me.'

'No, they are not and, yes, you do need something, but you just don't know it yet.'

'I could kick you,' she whispered, and his low rumble of laughter felt even more intimate than his warm hand in hers and the closeness of his powerful body.

'And fashionable people don't walk to masquerades, they are driven to them.'

'We are not fashionable people tonight and we're on our way to Vauxhall Gardens, not a private ball.'

'Don't people have to unmask at midnight?'

'Some of them can if they want to, but you don't have to,' he said. She could hear from the sternness in his voice that if anyone tried to make her they had him to reckon with. 'Just stop worrying and enjoy yourself, Lady Mel,' he added, and, since she didn't feel like hailing a hackney and dashing home in a huff, she decided she might as well.

'This is wonderful,' Melissa announced an hour or two later and looked around with the wide-eyed awe of a country girl confronted with the joys of city life. Adam thought she must have found it hard to get used to the din and pace of it all after the greenness and peace of the Shropshire countryside.

'So glad that you approve, my lady,' he said, and it was true. Despite the torture of having her so close and never close enough, he was enchanted by her enchantment. Her wonder at the brilliance and bustle and gaiety of the place seemed to have rubbed off on him and he saw it with new eyes.

'I would be hard to please if I didn't. The fireworks were wonderful and so pretty, and it must take such skill and knowledge to make them go off so smoothly one after the other like that. I wonder if there's a book about how they do it.'

'If there is I hope you don't try to make any. It

seems a dangerous trade at the best of times and I suspect the skills of it are a closely guarded family secret that gets passed down from one generation to the next.'

'Gunpowder and things,' she said wisely, and he tried not to find it enchanting that she took such a keen interest in the world around her. Most of the women he knew would have exclaimed at the dash and sparkle of it all and not given a second thought to how it was made or who had made it.

'Yes, unstable and explosive things,' he replied dourly.

'I have no intention of blowing my father's house up trying to make fireworks, Adam. I am only interested in how it's done, not in doing it myself,' she replied with a shake of the head and a gusty sigh, as if she couldn't imagine why he thought she would do such a thing.

That would be because he suspected she would dare anything if she thought it needed doing badly enough, or if she cared enough about whomever she was protecting at the time.

'Good, and I'm sorry I can't dance,' he said, and perhaps the champagne was a mistake. Melissa was so light-hearted and bright-eyed from it he couldn't regret his own small helping of it to keep her company, but he must keep a brake on his tongue somehow and remember this evening was meant to be a break from her cares and not a seduction.

'I prefer watching to being part of a crowd,' she said and eyed the revellers in front of the modest seats

he had secured for them, away from the boxes where
the rich and frivolous were growing more and more
rowdy as the night went on.

'Time we went,' he said with a weather eye on the
box where a group of young bucks were being rowdy.

'Must we?' asked the supposedly withdrawn and
self-contained Lady Melissa, as if she wanted to stay
out all night.

'Safer to leave before they start a brawl,' he said.
With a great deal more experience of wild young
bucks than she would ever have, he recognised a band
with enough brandy inside them to forget scruples
and inhibitions.

'I suppose so,' she conceded, and he had almost
pushed and shoved a way out for them when a very
drunken society buck lurched into their path.

'Here's a nice little pigeon ripe for the pluck-
ing,' the fool slurred out and wobbled as if his feet
were hardly capable of holding him up. 'Let's see
the goods, then,' he added, and Adam felt fury rise
like a spring tide when the sot reached for Melissa's
domino as if he was about to rip it off and humiliate
her in public.

He gripped the grinning fop's wrist so hard the
fool paled and looked a little sick when Adam twisted
it until he let the fabric go with a grunt of agony. As
well he had even that much sense, Adam decided
vengefully and leaned close enough to mutter a very
graphic threat about what he would do if the idiot took
one more step in the wrong direction.

'Come,' he said to Melissa and tugged her into a

dark corner before the fop's friends could round on him and leave her unprotected.

'Thank you,' she whispered as their rapid escape seemed to spark off the brawl he had felt brewing.

'We should have left half an hour ago,' he murmured as he searched his memory for the best way out without being caught in the melee. She had been so enthralled by the lights and music and merriment he didn't want to break the spell, and that made him stupid, or a besotted fool—neither felt attractive when he had her safety and peace of mind to consider.

'Oh, what a brute,' she whispered after giving a sympathetic 'Ouch!' for the next target of the entitled yahoos, and he was ashamed of having been one of them in his dizzy youth.

'Come on, we need to get you home before daybreak,' he said as lightly as he could, although his knowledge of the high spirits and curiosity of idle bucks said this could get far too serious and he had best get her away before it got nasty.

'We should stay and help the next victims,' she argued, tugging against his hand as he tried to get her to safety, and how right he was about the impulsive and headstrong nature under her pretend coolness. Their first meeting seemed a nice peaceful dream world as he pulled her after him willy-nilly and cursed himself for thinking he could show her some city life without risk of hurt or exposure. If they were caught and she was unmasked, the thought of the gossip if reclusive Lady Melissa was caught slumming with Limping Lord Lathbury made him shudder.

'Think how delighted your father's detractors will be if the constables are called and we have to admit who you are,' he muttered and felt her stop fighting and follow him willingly.

It wasn't until they were back in the relative safety of Mayfair that he dared relax and slow their pace to take account of the ache in his damaged knee. 'I should never have taken you there,' he murmured as she slowed her pace to match his halting one. He hated his infirmities when he thought what could have happened to her if he had not managed to hustle her out and scurry away in time to avoid fighting at least one drunken sot.

'Yes, you should. I had a wonderful time,' she argued robustly.

He thought of her delight in the fireworks and the music and laughter before she nearly had her mask ripped off by an idle young fool. 'Did you indeed?' he asked and revised his resolution never to put her in harm's way again. She had endured too much sheltering from harm these last few years from her family so this terror for such an innocent about the wider world was a price he would just have to pay.

'Yes, I did. Could a woman go masked to a play if she didn't want to be recognised?' she said with all the eagerness for all the pleasures she had been denying herself for so long in her voice, and he had better not think about all of those right now.

'Not without making you more noticeable than you are without one, but I dare say there are ways of disguising you if you truly want to go. Why not go openly, though? You must have cousins or aunts who would be happy to chaperon you on a visit to the theatre.'

'Can you imagine the stir it would cause if Lady Melissa sat in a box with even the most modest of parties? I can almost hear them whispering. *It's never her, you must have imagined it, but do let me have those opera glasses just to make sure.*'

Her bitter parody of a grande dame almost made him chuckle, except she sounded so bitter he hurt for her instead.

'And it would look like the thin end of the wedge to my father,' she went on. 'He would think I am about to relent and take my place in society and start having all sorts of wrong-headed ideas about my success.'

'You might well be one of those if you tried,' he said grumpily and felt as if lovely and restlessly intelligent Lady Melissa was even more distant from the likes of him than when they began their odd acquaintance.

'No, I never will. I can't imagine anything worse than having all those eyes focused on my every move,' she told him as if she truly meant it. 'But if you can get me into a theatre unnoticed I would really love to see a good play performed as I hear only London theatres can put them on.'

'Is that what you really want?' he asked, softening towards the idea as he sensed the genuine eagerness behind her odd request.

'Yes,' she told him with a little squirm of anticipation that said she thought she was being terribly daring to want to fulfil what sounded like a long-time wish.

He found her idea of a grand treat touchingly humble and knew he would have to find a way to make her wish come true. That meant forgetting his resolution to drop his self-torturing scheme to help her see more of the world around her and stop hiding in the tight little shell she had grown around herself at such a painfully young age she didn't even know what she was missing.

Chapter Thirteen

A heady mix of excitement, a little too much champagne and a snicker of fear for Adam when that brawl started and he had seemed ready to fight the world for her made Melissa feel she as if she had all the energy it took to keep walking at his side until daybreak. But she felt the halt in his step grow more pronounced and knew it was time they went home to their beds so he could rest. Tonight she wanted to be in his bed instead of hers even more than she did last night. Lord, what a shameless hussy she was and how good it felt to be alive and feeling so much she could hardly contain the hum and shimmer of excitement flowing through her veins.

Sensible Melissa had had to take the seat with her back to the horses when outrageous, wanton Melissa read that secret message from His Lordship here and decided they were going on this outing with him wherever it led. Now that her inner hussy was a bit castaway as well as wanton to her fingertips, she longed for him with every breath of sooty, smelly city air.

'There, we have got you home again safely and at long last,' he said softly, bending as close as a lover so there was no risk of them being overheard out here in the stilly watches of the night where she wanted to stay with him.

The possibilities and dangers of sensual tension stretched so fine between them that it felt as if it might break and cause mayhem as he bent over her in the shadow of the high garden wall. She opened her mouth in a sultry invitation to kiss without even thinking of rights and wrongs. She felt his clean breath on her pouting, wanting lips. Now he was so close she was triumphantly sure he had to kiss her before he finally gave in and bridged the gap between them.

She squirmed eagerly closer in a daze of sensuous relief that this time he wasn't going to back away from her and wish her a distant goodnight. He couldn't leave her longing and needy tonight as he had done in this very same place yesterday. He probably meant her to know he was going to kiss her witless this time, she thought, with a half-smile of tenderness for the mistaken gallantry of the man. He was giving her time and space to flinch away from him but why would she do that?

If he was less of a man, she might have been able to let him think he didn't matter to her, that his limp was the handicap he thought it was. Since he was this one she gave a soft sigh of relief and leaned back against that wall so he would lean in even closer and ravish her waiting mouth with kisses. It felt delicious to be so wrapped up in his hard male body again. It didn't matter if her legs refused to do their job and hold her up properly since he and this lovely wall would do it for her. The fire inside her shot to white heat as he kissed her as if she was crucial to his continued well-being, as if he needed her as much as his next breath.

It felt as if he had been hot and hungry for her since the moment their eyes met across that shadowed room the first night as well. She was so willing and fluid under his exploring hands she forgot to be ashamed of herself for wanting him so badly. She was so glad he shifted them about without stopping their kiss and letting common sense flood back in. Now he was the one with his back to a hard wall and she was even more open to his exploring touch in the shadows, and how dearly she needed his hands on her, urgent and strong and just like that.

She was starving for the wondering touch he ran over her feminine curves, then he rested his hands on her backside as if it felt like the perfect place for them to be for him as well, and heat raged inside her. And now he was busy with the ties of her round gown. His hands shook and showed her vulnerability as well as power, need as well as wanting. He took his mouth away from her hungry one long enough to slick the chord of her neck with kisses and follow the gap he had created until he found where her silky chemise met the full swell of an aching breast with his tongue.

She had to bite her lip to stifle a moan of sensuous

delight. Reminded they were in the street in the middle of the night by the noise she had almost let out, she still could not call a halt and pretend to be outraged or the innocent party. She was so hungry for his touch, so desperate for his mouth to sink that bit lower and seize her eager nipple in his mouth and suckle on it until she didn't care where they were and what time of day it was for the sheer outrageous pleasure of it.

'We can't.' He raised his head to whisper shakily in her ear and even that only made her want him more. The feel of his accelerated breathing against that workaday organ made her not want to listen to his words, but long to feel his tongue exploring the curlicues and sensuality of newly sensitive skin. Then he could lick and kiss his way down the side of her neck and they were back to the pebble-hard ache of her craving nipples and if only they were. If only he would let his mouth dip and find the tingling, throbbing needy welcome he would find there as he finally forgot to be so confoundedly noble.

'You err,' she finally managed to mumble grumpily as he still held off from that longed-for, giddying pleasure that would surely take her beyond willing and on to ravenous for everything they could have with one another. He was using his hands to hold her a little bit away from all the potential glory she wanted so badly and he apparently did not want as much, but he could not walk away from her anyway.

'We *can*, but you won't let us,' she added bleakly. Correct and cautious Lady Melissa forced her way through and screamed at her sensual other half that she was a blind little fool who deserved to be locked in the nearest dungeon until she had learnt to be quiet if she could not be good. Her weak and wanton inner idiot still longed for him so badly it felt as if something terrible might happen if she didn't have him, but he wasn't going to give her the choice. He was distancing himself from her with far more than space and it hurt so much she was almost ready to wish she had never met him.

'No, I won't let you make love in the street like a bangtail with a client,' he told her gruffly and as if the burn and frustration of saying no to this cost him dear, but what would it have cost her if he wasn't better at remembering the world than she was?

'Oh, no,' she said as shock ripped through her. Of course that was what she had wanted, what she was silently begging him for in order to sate hot needs and dreamy desires that were knotting up the core of her with silken bonds. She was as wild and reckless and every bit as wicked as the shocked tabbies at Wiston Veryan had sworn she was when she was sixteen and rode bareback about the countryside in man's breeches and did whatever she thought would shock them, until that lie about her eloping for Gretna with an unsuitable rogue got out to thrill them all. If they knew what she had really done they would have decided she was a she-devil, a wicked destroyer of a good boy's life.

Memory of that time brought her back down to earth with a sickening thump. Reminded that her son must never be found because her sins would fall down on his innocent life like a ton of bricks that would stifle him, she flinched away from her fiery inner rebel and what she had been inviting so wantonly.

'Let me go,' she demanded flatly. She wanted to hide away, go back to the countryside and lose herself in some anonymous place where she could start a blank and respectable life anew. The most remote place on her father's estate was impossible since she had gone there when she was growing Joe's baby in her belly, then birthed him without a father or a wedding ring. And hiding wouldn't unknot the shameful twist of need that still whispered how much she would miss this very different man if she never saw him again.

She should not want to see him again so badly or have this bleak hollow in her heart at the thought of never knowing another thing about him. Never seeing him again, never longing for his touch and all the delicious intimacy they could have had if only she was different felt like a bleak punishment for her wayward youth, but she would learn to bear it; she had already endured so much bleak separation from those she loved one more ought to be easy, but something told her this one could break her if she let it.

'No, marry me,' Adam said much too seriously.

For a moment she let herself dream it could be, that she could spend the rest of her life with this brave, wounded and magnificent man. Then the truth crept back in and she knew she could not wed him or anyone else. According to church and state she was a lost and fallen woman, so even if he loved her he couldn't marry her. And she could not do him such a backhanded turn.

Marriage to anyone but her dead love was something she had turned her back on when they made their baby all those lonely years ago and that was that. She could not marry Adam if they were found naked in Grosvenor Square together by the fashionable crowd about to set off for Rotten Row and their daily melee of seeing and being seen.

'I shall never marry and I certainly won't marry you,' she told him as if she was furious at the very idea, even as she had to blink back tears for the glorious might-have-been she was throwing away.

'You have a very individual way of showing your indifference to suitors, Lady Melissa,' he said coldly. The distance between them began to seem like yards rather than a few careful inches. 'I wonder they do not besiege you in droves if that's the sort of welcome you lay out before sending them away with a flea in their ear.'

'They can try, but I won't receive them, or you.'

'I am the only one who knows about you, so they are not going to call on you with flowers and pleas for mercy,' he said flatly.

That stubborn isolation and all her secrets stacked up to make her nod silently in the dark and bitterly acknowledge he was right. He did know her a bit too well already and she could not endure the idea of having to tell all her secrets.

'I still won't marry you,' she told him. The temptation to say nothing about her past loves and losses and let him damn himself with such a wife made her sound harsh and angry, but if it made him step away from her then that was good.

'Never is a long time. Right now I'm for my bed, my lady. I'm too old and still too proud to stand and argue my case any further tonight when we can do it all again in the morning in comfort and after a good night's sleep.'

'Don't you dare call and ask my father for his permission to marry me. I will never forgive you if you do so. In fact, I shall go back to the country and make sure you never see me again if you even try to force your will on me in such an infamous way.'

'I should wait until you are asked before you fire up and run away, Melissa mine,' he whispered, then limped off into the night as if the first half of that sentence didn't argue with the second.

'Weasel!' she hissed after him and thought she heard a faint chuckle—of all the things the wretch could have thrown back at her. She knew he wasn't far away, that he was waiting for her to go inside and shut the door behind her. He was waiting for her to be safe when she felt as if she was never going to be safe from her wicked, wanton, feral self ever again while Adam Lathbury was vibrant and alive and far too desirable for wayward ladies who ought to avoid him like the plague.

Somehow she managed not to slam the garden door behind her and defy his care for her undeservedly spotless reputation. Using the key she'd pocketed earlier, she crept through the side door and tiptoed past the night watchman snoring in the hall. She took the back stairs and padded up on bare feet and finally let herself into her splendid suite through the service door of the dressing room. A night creeper would be proud of her. She sat down on her splendid bed and sighed for the lover who wasn't here to admire her stealth or glory in the peace and quiet of my lady's feather bed and pristine sheets as they rumpled and jumbled them in their hot and hasty desire.

'No good, wanton Melissa,' she whispered regretfully. 'He's never going to happen to you now.' She sat in silence replaying the events of the night with all its light and darkness, and hope and bitterness. 'Oh, Adam, however am I going to live without you?' she whispered in the silvery shaft of moonlight that had suddenly come out from behind the clouds. At least he would be back home and in his bedchamber as well by now so nobody would see my lord picked out in the moonlight on the way home from a shady assignation. She managed to stumble out of her clothes and fold the plain gown and hide it at the bottom of a chest. Nobody would miss it and she could never wear it again without regretting Adam as her lover since he could never be her husband, and she regretted him even more.

With a heartfelt sigh she climbed into bed, feeling as if the world had shifted all over again, and told herself exactly why she could never marry Adam. Her boy, she reminded herself with another terrible ache inside that seemed about to burst out of her and scream for the sheer emptiness of her life. Her beloved baby she so dearly hoped was a sturdy, happy boy by now, eager for life and the wide world opening ahead of him.

She still had to find that letter somehow and make sure all that promise held true for her son and her sins never caught up with him. But just for this empty, grievous moment she could let herself cry for all the days she had never had with him and add on the ones she would have to live without him *and* the big-hearted, unique man who could have been the second love of her life. She lay down at last and allowed herself to cry just this once. Her pillow was wet with tears and she had to muffle hiccuping sobs in it lest someone heard her and came to see what the matter was. She knew there was no comfort to be had as loss made her curl into a hurting ball until exhaustion took her under at last and she slept.

All too soon it was morning again and it felt bitterly familiar as Melissa woke up, knowing she had seen the last of Adam. This one felt even more bleak and empty as she rubbed her gritty eyes and tried to shake some clarity into her aching head. Despite her resolution to let go of even the idea of him as a lover, somehow she missed him so much it hurt. How different she would feel now if she was free to wake up with him beside her and rampant and eager for her, and never mind how long Ellen had to wait to come in and get Her Ladyship ready to face the day.

It could even be tomorrow before her husband let her out of it if he was only possible and here and her vast and stately bed didn't feel empty and, oh, so cold without him in it. Calling herself all sorts of an idiot, she rang the bell and tried to face life as it was and definitely not cry about it like a watering pot.

'Fellow sent round a letter for you,' her father informed her when he found her in his library trying to clear her aching head before she searched the books and papers Adam had sent round only yesterday, even if it did feel half a world further away than that.

'What fellow?' she said warily.

'Lathbury, of course—what other fellow do you know who would send you letters as if he has a right? Anyway, you had best see what he has to say,' the Duke said with his politics face on after that grumpy outburst, so she had no idea what he really thought of Adam's visit yesterday, or the one her father knew about anyway. She hated to think of him finding out about the second one and leaping to the wrong conclusion about that late-night assignation.

'Oh, very well,' she said with what she hoped was a weary sigh of pretend patience for a gentleman who had used one encounter in the Park to scrape an acquaintance.

I expect to hear by this evening whether you have found what you seek or not.

That was what he'd written and did not even add his signature or words of greeting or farewell. Apparently she was in disgrace with him, but not completely cut off, so it was all to do again. Why wouldn't the noble great idiot give up on her? She had refused to marry him after seeming all too willing to be seduced last night before reality hit her and she realised it was impossible. He ought to hate her and be revolted by her blowing hot and cold and simply go away and leave her to nurse her headache and heartache in peace.

'Oh, I see,' she said, and her father raised his eyebrows to argue he certainly did not. 'He has heard nothing back from his fellow buyers at the auction yet,' she lied lamely.

'And he considers it urgent to tell you precisely nothing and send a messenger around to tell you about it?'

'Apparently so.'

'I would have put money on Lathbury being a tougher nut to crack than the rest of the fools who would line up to marry you if you would only let them see you,' the Duke said as if he had read the sensual attraction humming between that noble lord and his daughter far too easily and now he was even more worried about her than usual.

'You know I shall never marry, Papa. Lord Lathbury is intent on trying to right a wrong, and we have only met twice and the second time was in your presence.'

'It took me two seconds to decide your mother was the only woman for me.'

'That was exceptional. Everyone knows you two had a love match, and you know I cannot have one of those after what happened when I was young.' It would have been wonderful to share one with Adam in some other fairyland. In the real world she had loved Joe first so there wasn't even a chance of a happy ending for her now.

'It's a father's duty to want the best for his child, whatever she believes to the contrary,' her father told her.

'I know, Papa, and I really do love you.'

'Good, good, now get on and search those papers and we will just have to hope that Lathbury comes up with a good answer from the other collectors if that confounded letter isn't in there somewhere.'

By the end of the afternoon Melissa was weary and her eyes ached even more than they had when she woke up. She had found her grandparents' correspondence with their learned friends and lots of family letters Cousin Vernon should never have included in a public auction, but not the one that could give away her dearest secret. She penned a brief message to His Lordship informing him she had searched the papers, but he would have to give her more time to search every book he had given her, then she sent it to Lathbury House without any polite formalities either. Did he mean to storm in here and challenge her in person if she didn't reply in time? Now she just wanted to find the letter and get back some sort of peace.

Tired and depressed after searching through those papers and an even harder night slamming into the truth of life without Adam Lathbury, she retired to her room early that night with a headache and even drank the tisane Ellen brought her in the hope it might allow her a few hours of peaceful sleep. Adam had not sent her any more impudent messages so he must have accepted her no as final after all. Melissa had never felt more hopeless as she contemplated her search without Adam to make it more of an adventure than the desperate undertaking it was. Still, he was a fantasy and her son was real. She was all that stood between her boy and shame and acrimony. Whatever it took, she would keep standing here and keep on looking for that letter until she found it.

Chapter Fourteen

'His Grace wishes to see you, Lady Melissa. His Grace is in the library,' the butler informed her the following afternoon.

'Again?' she could not help saying and could only think of one reason why her father would call her down to the library in the middle of the day.

'Yes, my lady.'

'Very well, but please tell him that I will be ten minutes.'

She was not going downstairs dusty and dressed in an old gown if it did happen to be Adam come to find out what she had found among these endless-seeming books. He would just have to wait if it was him. She had only just finished her task and come upstairs to change, and she was not going back down again looking like this. They might be finished as anything more than acquaintances, but she did have some pride.

* * *

It was more like a quarter of an hour before she was washed and changed and Ellen had brushed all the dust out of her hair and rearranged it. Melissa thought that was quick, considering the state she had been in when she came up to get rid of her dirt. And all the while her heart was beating faster and lighter than usual and it was an effort to keep her breathing steady under Ellen's sharp scrutiny.

And she was right; it was him, but who else would it be? No other man would boldly walk into Wiston House when she was known to be a social recluse. Nobody else would look quite so unabashed after they parted on her refusal to even think about marrying him, even if they had been even more carried away by passion than they were.

Her father and Adam seemed stiff and rather ill at ease together when she joined them in the library, and she wondered what they had found to talk about while they waited for her. It felt like a peculiar repeat of his last visit here, except there were even more crates of books and yet another document box in a pile on the luxurious Turkey carpet the poor maids had only just managed to clean after the last of Grandmama's books were repacked in their crates and borne off to the attic until Melissa had worked out what to do with them.

'Ah, there you are at last, my dear. Lathbury was determined to speak to you in person and I suppose it concerns this latest set of books from that confounded auction, but I am expected in Downing Street shortly. I will have to leave you to it. Doing that once makes me a bad enough father and twice is getting to be a habit, Lathbury.

'I am a busy man and we will need to send for one of my aunts or cousins to keep my daughter in countenance if you are going to be calling on her so regularly. I could resign from the Government, I suppose, but it would feel like deserting a sinking ship,' her father said with a look of concern from Adam to her as if he sensed something deeper than a mutual interest in books to His Lordship's second call at Wiston House by daylight.

Despite his obvious reservations, her father gave Melissa a preoccupied kiss farewell and shot Adam a ducal frown of warning and added an exhortation not to keep her long, then he hurried out just in time for his carriage to appear from the mews. She heard him order the coachman to whip 'em up because he was damnably late before the front door closed behind him, and she felt as if the subsequent silence had too many listening ears in it for comfort.

'I don't want one of my great-aunts or my father's tiresome cousin Augusta living here and making our lives a misery, Lord Lathbury, so please stop calling on me and save us that particular hardship,' she told Adam stiffly.

'Are you intending to cultivate a wider acquaintance?' he asked as if he was only mildly interested in her answer.

'No,' she said curtly.

'Then if I promise to visit only when I have more books to hand over there is no need for you to acquire a chaperon or for the government to collapse without your father's help.'

'Indeed?' she said distantly and allowed herself a quiet sigh of relief as she heard Carnforth's footsteps retreat to his butler's pantry until she rang the bell. They must sound like faintly hostile acquaintances then and that was something, wasn't it?

'Yes, now come down off your high horse, Your Ladyship, and kindly promise me something in return.'

'Why should I?'

'Because these are the lots that Spilling bought at that confounded auction and I require the same promise about them as I managed to wring out of you about my own lots.'

'He had all these?' she asked, and the task she had thought was over and done with at least for today was not over with at all, and he was manipulating her into not going out to find them herself.

'Yes. I went to see him while you were busy with my part of it yesterday. Since Spilling has the poor taste to live twenty miles out of London it took a while to get them here, but since he had not unpacked them it was more straightforward than it could have been.'

'But...' She lost the power of speech for a moment, gulped and tried again. 'But you cannot do such a thing for a stranger,' she managed to protest this time.

'Wrong, my lady; for one thing you are not one of those and for another I just have.'

'You shouldn't have gone to all that trouble on my

account and they must have cost you dear to buy and transport so quickly,' she made herself protest, although she was so relieved, her legs were wobbling. She badly wanted to throw her arms round his neck and kiss him, but that was forbidden and wrong, and she wasn't sure she wanted him to go on protecting her from the worst aspects of this search or go away and leave her to get on with it alone.

Stay, her inner siren argued. *No, make him go away*, the rest of her argued sternly.

No wonder Adam was watching her warily and as if he could read her mad inner argument from her tense frown and hungry mouth.

'Sir Horace Spilling is a terrible old roué and I knew you would have gone yourself if I hadn't got there first. At least I had already managed to make sure you were too busy to dash into Surrey yourself and beat me to it.'

'Then that's why you insisted I had to look through your papers straight away? You just wanted me out of the way.'

'The idea of you breaking into Spilling's library at midnight dressed as a boy made me go cold right down to my bones. It would lead to disaster one way or another, and please don't try to argue you wouldn't have done it because I know perfectly well that you would. I think you would walk into hell itself and fight the devil for whatever you are looking for if you had to. I did what I had to do to stop you having to fight off Spilling or be arrested for housebreaking. Now it's your turn to get to work and find out if your secret is safe in there somewhere or if it is all to do again with the next man on the list of buyers.'

'No, you can't keep doing this, Adam. It must have cost you so much to get these, and please don't try to convince me you didn't have to pay Sir Horace more than they cost him because I won't believe you. This is my quest and I must cover the cost of it.' She saw barely contained fury in his hot gaze and set mouth, and her stupid knees wobbled again because she had hurt him again. She didn't want to, but how else was she going to persuade him he must leave her alone?

'Think of it as a price I could not let you pay. What sort of man would I be if I sat at home and waited to read about your arrest for burglary in the news-sheets, Melissa?'

'A good one who has done quite enough for a complete stranger already.'

'I am just a *stranger* to you?' he asked with a bitter emphasis.

'A friend, then,' she corrected herself. Even having one of those would have warmed a cold piece of her heart if only that was all he was to her.

'No,' he said with a sigh that sounded weary and sad. 'A person trusts a friend and you don't trust anyone, do you?'

'No, that's wrong; I do trust you. I trust you completely, Adam,' she was shocked into arguing as she saw hurt behind his anger. 'But you are an honourable man. How could I ask you to break into another man's library with me and try to steal what I am looking for when you could so easily be arrested along with me?'

'Dammit, woman, my nanny retired years ago and I don't need a replacement.'

'Don't swear at me, and I didn't mean to hurt your pride,' she said stiffly.

'Ah, pride,' he said with a dismissive gesture. 'If you think that's all I have to lose here I must be even poorer at expressing myself than I thought I was.'

'Then please don't.'

'Don't what?'

'Express yourself better.'

'Not here and not now,' he said tersely and found a way to pace her father's library despite all the crates piled up in it and that very correct open door. 'I will have the truth out of you one day, my lady, and a reckoning for it between us straight afterwards.'

'I would be quite grateful for one right now, my lord,' she told him stiffly. 'I can afford whatever inflated price you had to pay Sir Horace Spilling for my books and papers.'

'Be grateful you're not a man, Lady Melissa, so I don't have to call you out for that insult. You didn't ask me to buy the cursed books, so kindly accept them with at least a semblance of grace and give me the promise I asked for.'

'Why should I?'

Because I will run mad worrying about what you are up to if that damned secret of yours is not here, of course, Adam silently argued with her.

How could he say it out loud when she wanted to

treat him like some passing acquaintance she had met for the first time in the Park one fine morning?

'Who knows? For the sake of my sanity perhaps, or to stop me keeping watch on this house night and day so I know you can't leave it for the next library on your list without me knowing? Who knows or cares why? Just promise you will tell me if you find what you are looking for and be done with it, my lady.'

He heard the edge of desperation in his own voice and took up limping again although he knew he ought to leave. They were alone in here even with the door wide open and Wiston's butler far too well-trained and discreet to let them know he might be listening.

It had been more than the twenty minutes some unwritten law laid down for a morning call and he was still here. He wasn't going to go away until she promised to tell him if she found what she wanted, either. That way he would have time to get to Mayburn before she could and bring the last of her stolen property back before the man had a chance to look through it in detail and she had a chance to get herself in more trouble without him.

'You might as well give me that promise because I won't go without it,' he said softly as he ground to a halt again beside her because of Carnforth's carefully not listening ears. 'It's not much to ask, one stranger to another,' he added bitterly and could have kicked himself when he saw her withdraw even further into the stiff pose he now knew was her refuge from hurt.

Curse it, he could have endless patience with a nervous horse or an abused dog when he was trying to

win their trust, but this woman meant far too much
to him and he didn't seem to have a patient bone in
his body any longer.

Because she could hurt him too easily by not trust-
ing him, he kept falling over his own tongue. He
should be deft and patient with her until she trusted
him enough not to hurt her. But she had felt so wondrous and fluid and responsive when he kissed her.
Before she panicked, she had responded with all the
ardour and pent-up emotion he had sensed in her from
the very first look. Now he went back to his pacing so
she wouldn't see what just the memory of her, warm
and wonderful in his arms, did to him.

'Oh, very well,' Melissa agreed at last because he
was stubborn enough to stay here until she gave in.
Her father's servants were highly trained and well
paid to be discreet, given Papa's political service, but
they were still human. They were sure to gossip if
Lord Lathbury spent much longer here arguing with
her when her father was absent and not even the whisper of a chaperon to be seen.

'I promise...?' he trailed and took out his watch to
watch the minutes tick well beyond what was proper
even if they had that chaperon.

'I promise to tell dictatorial, sly, stubborn Lord Lathbury if I find what I am looking for in this latest pile
of books and papers,' she said through gritted teeth.

'Excellent. Well then, I really must go now,' he said
cheerfully and as if she had kept him waiting far too
long already. Then he put his half-hunter back into

his pocket and said, 'Good day to you, Lady Melissa, and happy reading.'

He didn't even bother to kiss her anywhere unexpected and shiveringly wonderful; he simply bowed and left the room as if it had only ever been a polite morning call. She heard him thank Carnforth for his hat and cane and listened to Adam's slightly halting step in the marble hallway, then out of the door and down the elegant stone steps until Carnforth shut the door behind him.

She was left staring at this latest pile of books and she sighed because the rest of the day and most of tomorrow would now be taken up with them. Happy reading indeed! The wretch, how dare he say that and then walk away? She rang for the handyman to come and remove the nails from the lid of the crates and tried to divert herself from missing Adam by wondering where on earth they would put so many books when she was done.

While she worked out where she was going to live one day, at least she would not be thinking of impossible things with the man who had delivered them, then demanded her promise to stay at home and search through them. Without Adam anywhere in her life, or her child or anything that looked like hope, it looked like a very bleak future indeed, so no wonder she buried it in a flurry of driven activity and forgot to consider what came next.

Chapter Fifteen

Melissa found another terse message inside the latest box of documents. It ordered her to meet Adam the following night in the usual place. She burnt it and sent back an equally terse reply, sealed with her father's seal so nobody would know it came from her. What would the one word *No*, written in broad, angry strokes, tell anyone else, anyway? Not that it mattered since *No* did not seem to be in His Lordship's vocabulary.

The wretch turned up the following afternoon with three volumes of a brand-new novel by 'A Lady' he thought she might enjoy, looking as if he ought to be as welcome as the flowers in spring. Although she was still weary from searching all the books, her back ached and she did not bother to change this time before she found out what he wanted, very annoyingly he still was that welcome in secret even as she greeted him with a frown.

'You promised not to call again,' she said to hide the fact she was so glad he had not listened that even the air felt lighter under her feet because he was here.

'I said I would only come when I had books for you and these are definitely books, Lady Melissa. I have quite a few of them in my library and I recognise them on sight now.'

'These are not the books you meant.'

'How do you know?'

'Oh, just go away, you exasperating man,' she demanded, and only just managed to suppress a smile.

'Very well, then, but first I need an answer.'

'I have not heard a question yet.'

She met his gaze fully for the first time and saw more than mischief there; there was a warmth and a steadfast purpose that ought to have made her wary when he handed her the first volume after he had shifted the paper slipped inside the cover until it was visible.

I can always come to the front door at the usual time if you prefer to be open about our acquaintance.

If she was expecting him to beg forgiveness for summoning her like a sheepdog she was going to be disappointed.

'No!' she gasped, all the shocking implications of him openly calling on a lady at that time of night hitting her with appalled clarity. 'You can't do that.'

'Then kindly do as I asked you to and turn up tonight if you don't want me to stand out in the back road and howl,' he said as if he might do just that if she didn't.

She told herself she was bowing to the inevitable when she nodded, because she could not bring herself to say 'yes' out loud and let him win every hand they played. 'Why?' she demanded before he could look smug about it.

'Because you need to see more of the world before you reject it again, my lady,' he said as if it really was that simple.

'No, I don't, and what if we're caught?'

'We won't be. You will make sure the world thinks you are safely tucked up in bed and my sister and grandmother will be out until dawn,' he said as if he didn't quite approve of her caution or terror of them being found out.

The heedless hoyden of old would think it was wonderful for her to be caught in a very compromising situation with Lord Lathbury so she had no choice but to marry him in order to save his reputation. She told herself she had stopped listening to the reckless little devil a long time ago. He was right; she could make very sure the whole household realised she was very weary indeed after her battle with all these books His Lordship would keep bringing her and that she was not to be disturbed on any account until late tomorrow morning.

'Until tonight, then, my Lady Mel,' he whispered in her ear and kissed it instead of her neck this time.

She was too busy trying to stop her breath audibly

gasping for more and her knees from wobbling her closer to him for her to have the nous to say anything else as he bowed a pretending-to-be-formal farewell and gave her a satisfied grin. Then he was on his way after spending less than five minutes in her father's house.

How could anyone guess he had very personal business with her when he had stayed such a short space of time? she asked herself as she put her hand to her aching lips and missed him like…like…well, like, him, she supposed. Nothing as tempting and forbidden and impossible as Adam Lathbury occurred to her to compare him with and that was even more worrying.

It was nearly noon when Melissa stirred after another surreptitious night with Adam. She smiled and stretched luxuriously in her very comfortable bed and decided he was very good at his mission to let fun and laughter into her life, even if he had become a complete miser with his kisses. Last night he had smuggled her into the theatre dressed in a grey wig and an enveloping cap to pretend she was his elderly aunt out for a rare treat. She watched with countrified awe as the gossiping and laughter of the farce gave way to the engrossing drama of Shakespeare's *Tempest*, and all the shape changing and magic and deception must have followed her home and got into her dreams.

If only she had magic at her fingertips to make herself a happy ending, she thought wistfully. For once she dreaded having that letter safely in her hand, then into the fire so it could never haunt her with its painful truth writ large ever again. Stupid of her to think having it in her hand even for a brief moment before she destroyed it could undo the past. She would never wish her child unmade, not even for Adam's sake and for all the things they could be to one another if she wasn't a fallen woman. Instead she must remember and cling to Joe's and their baby's memory instead of holding out any hope of a future with Adam.

No sooner had she made that stern resolution than she was daydreaming about the man once again, as if stern and realistic Melissa had never given the rest of her that strict lecture. She pictured him at the social occasions he felt he must attend with his sister and grandmother and was horribly, burningly jealous of every second he spent in the company of the socially adept, confident and flirtatious beauties of the *ton*.

Melissa sat up in bed and forgot to be languorous and dreamy-eyed about him as the reality of who he was sank in once again. He was still handsome and intriguing and very marriageable. And not all debutantes and established beauties were fools; they would see for themselves how desirable Lord Lathbury was as a husband and lust after him as well as his fortune and title. If he must sit to chat, sip warm wine and fan overheated ladies at debutantes' balls, he ought to do it with her. For the first time in over a decade she longed for the high life and all the elegant diversions of the Season because if he was at them she wanted to be there.

'Stupid, stupid, stupid woman,' she raged at herself for even thinking about him like that.

She hastily rang the bell so she could don her least favourite gown, ask Ellen to dress her hair practically and severely, and busy herself with the task she had been putting off for so long. She was going to sort through the jumble of discarded furniture and old clothes in the vast attics even the number of servants it took to run this large house could not fill. Then there would be room for the crates of books currently cluttering up Papa's library because all the gaps there had been were already full of the first lot.

She had been through every one of the new ones and found a laundry list, a few adverts for long-forgotten lectures used as bookmarks and a recipe for violet hair powder she could not imagine was ever a good idea, even when her grandmother was young and reputed to be as lovely as she was clever.

After a hasty and very late breakfast Melissa was directing as many footmen and maids as could be spared from other duties to move and sweep and clean things up in the attics when the butler appeared, and her troops were probably smothering a collective sigh of relief at the interruption.

'The Duke...a caller, my lady,' Carnforth explained breathlessly.

'Again?'

'Indeed, my lady,' he replied with a repressive look at his underlings to say get on with your work and don't question the peculiar ways of your employers.

'Ellen, please have warm water brought to my room,' Melissa said as calmly as she could when her heart was beating as fast as poor Carnforth's probably was after the long climb up here to find her, since she had commandeered the servants he could have sent instead.

'Don't say anything,' she ordered her maid a few minutes later as Ellen carefully removed the dust-and-cobweb-strewn cap from Melissa's hair and set about brushing it free of any stray ones, then making her look like a proper lady again.

'No, my lady,' Ellen said with pretend meekness, but she still insisted on removing Melissa's dusty petticoat before she could throw the gown that had just been sent round by the dressmaker over a new one so Melissa was clean and fashionable when she joined Adam in her father's library.

This time Papa had not even waited for her before he left for whatever business he had to conduct at the House, and she wondered if he was getting those wild ideas about her and Adam again when he ought to know it was impossible.

'More books?' she asked Adam, staring at a new stack of packing cases forced to the edges of the room since she hadn't managed to clear space in the attics for the last lot yet.

'I believe that's the end of the auction lots, apart from the fine illustrated volumes sold one by one, and they were picked over before the sale so if they had held any secrets they would be out in the open by now.'

She was glad she had made sure her grandmother's most precious illustrated books were carefully packed away to distract herself from her grief after her grandmother died and Vernon informed her women had no place at funerals. There was nothing significant hidden in any of them and she felt a twinge of regret for the meticulous beauty of some of the finely painted colour plates and a book of hours she would never see the like of again, but they were gone and there were more important things for her to regret than a few hand-coloured books, however beautiful they might be.

'Thank you so much,' she said and gave him a helpless shrug to say what else could she say when he would not let her pay him back. 'There are even more of them than last time,' she added. All the searching and hoping still to do made her feel weary, but this was her last hope of finding that letter. She would find the energy from somewhere, but what if it wasn't here? What then? Terror made her heart race and she made herself breathe deeply and not show it.

'If only we could smuggle them out at night as well as you, we could search together,' he said with a concerned look and as if he knew how she felt anyway.

'Hush!' she said hastily and with a furtive glance towards the correctly open again door out into the hall, since she was a single lady meeting with a single gentleman and without even her father to lend them countenance this time. And she would never let Adam see that damning, revealing letter. The very thought of him watching her with contempt instead of veiled amusement as the truth of who and what she was sank in made her blood run cold.

'Maybe I am tired of hiding in the dark, my lady,' he challenged her without even bothering to murmur, and evidently he was.

'I must find my letter,' she said with an annoyingly helpless look to plead for time to go through all these books and papers before he threw down whatever challenge he was working up to this time. If she had enough time, she might find a way to stop him throwing it down at all. She knew that if she told him the truth he was honourable enough to keep her secrets, but she could not bring herself to do it and never see him again. Yet again she was being a coward and she despised herself even as she eyed him warily and longed for another night in the dark with him and London to explore all around them and nobody the wiser.

'Oh, aye, that's more important to you than I am.'

'Not more important, just different,' she told him as calmly as she could with all the conflicting emotions of mother and lover and whatever he was to her battling for supremacy inside her like a nest full of angry hornets, and now she didn't even have to cry to give herself a headache over him.

'More important,' he corrected her flatly. She stayed silent and he took it as confirmation. He turned on his heel and was halfway across the room before he turned back to bark words at her as if he wanted the whole world to know he was feeling angry and impatient. 'I will give you three days to find it, Melissa. Then I'll have an answer from you one way or another,' he said over his shoulder before he marched out of the room.

She gazed after him, feeling shocked and adrift in a suddenly unstable world. Part of her wanted to run after him, say yes to the question he hadn't even asked her, whatever it was. She would expose her confused and turbulent feelings for the man to the eyes of the world once and for all if she did and she couldn't do that, could she? She couldn't let him say it, or ask her anything unless he knew the truth. And how could she tell him that without risking her son's happiness and a whole lifetime's worth of peace of mind?

It took mere seconds for the sound of Adam's slight limp to clear the marble floor of the hall this time. He thanked Carnforth tersely for his hat and cane and was outside with the door closed behind him before she could dash to one of the long windows looking on to the Square and watch my Lord Lathbury stride away in a grand temper.

'What's this?' the Duke of Wiston asked his daughter when they sat down after dinner later that day and he saw the first volume of the novel Adam had given her on the table by her favourite chair in the little sitting room where they sat when her father was not engaged for the evening.

Fighting her confused feelings for Adam, she hoped to distract herself from his three-day ultimatum by reading it. At least she didn't need to pretend more weariness than she felt tonight since Adam would not be summoning her for any more evenings of adventure and discovery with him. The novel he had given her was written with subtle humour and a rather wicked perception of human folly, but it would be asking too much of even a Shakespeare play performed in their own house by the best actors of this generation to hold her attention for long tonight.

'It doesn't look like your usual sort of reading,' her father added.

'No, but it is amusing and insightful and I believe you would enjoy it when I finish with the first volume. I shall not give it up lightly even for you now I have begun it.'

'I admit I'm astonished you found the time to visit a bookshop or that you felt the need for any more books than the ones Lathbury has been sending you by the cartload.'

'You know he is only being a gallant gentleman who feels it is his duty to right a wrong now he realises the books were sold illegally. Anyway, I didn't buy it,' she said and pretended to be searching for the paper knife so she could cut the next few pages in order to hide her blushes. 'Lord Lathbury gave it to me. Apparently he has read this novel by a lady and thought I would enjoy it, and it turns out that he is quite right.'

'He's a cunning devil, I'll give him that much. You said he had promised not to call on you unless he brought you more books and that is what he's done every time he has been here so far. I can't fault his strategy.'

'I suppose not.'

'You must be the last person in this house to know Lathbury is courting you with books,' her father said as if he didn't quite know what to think of the idea.

'Of course he isn't,' she said uneasily, so glad he didn't know about her late-night excursions with Adam to add to his worries about her and where this might lead if she let it.

'I might be old and only your father, but I'm not quite a fool, Mel. Lathbury obviously means business and you must decide how important he is to you and how much you can trust him. You risk being badly hurt again if you cannot tell him what he needs to know and he tries to court you in public as well as private.'

'And what if I find out I dare not trust him enough to tell him the truth?'

'Then you must end it, once and for all. Make it crystal clear to him there is no future in him persisting with this campaign of his to somehow get my daughter out into the light and into his arms after all these years of solitude and brooding over a past that cannot be altered, however much both of us long for it to have had a different outcome for you.'

'You make it sound as if that's what you want him to do.'

'Of course I do, I'm your father and I love you.'

'You know better than anyone else why it's a terrible idea for me to be deeply involved with any man, let alone Adam Lathbury.'

'Only if he doesn't love you enough to accept you as you are, then and now.'

'How could he, Papa? How could a proud man like Adam Lathbury ever live with a wife he did not respect?'

'I shall certainly not respect him if he fails to understand why you did what you did when you were so painfully young and I was so absorbed in my own selfish grief for your mother I didn't even wonder where you kept getting off to when you were meeting young Joseph Briggs. I shall never forgive myself for making you turn to the one person in your life who worried about your feelings and your grief and loneliness instead of me. The lad was there for you when I let you down, but when I found out what you two had done together before he died I was so furious I couldn't even look at you.

'If I had, I would have seen your mother in you and realised she would have hated me for what I had done to her beloved daughter. So, I made you hide yourself away all alone while the rest of us spun a Banbury tale about your frustrated elopement so you could just about retain your good name. You didn't have anyone at all because it was so much easier for me to act the outraged father in London while you were supposed to be abroad with your grandparents and enjoying an undeserved Grand Tour.

'Yet there you were, hiding like a ghost all alone but for your ancient nanny while you waited for your child to be born and then taken away from you. The life you have lived these last ten years is proof I was even more wrong to have insisted on parting you from your child. Anything would feel better than knowing you live like a hermit because of my failings. At least your way would have meant you could see the lad grow and I could have visited you both now and again.'

'You were right, though; my son was too like me not to be mine,' she said with the old blank misery welling up inside her as she recalled her delight in her baby and her horror when he was born looking so much like her it was unmistakable. She knew there was no pretending he was some distant Aldercombe cousin's orphaned child when he bore her stamp so unmistakably. 'I so wanted him to look like Joe it's no wonder I cried when he was born.'

'I know you did. I was there, don't forget,' he reminded her painfully, and thank heaven he had been. Maybe the heartbreak of her situation had finally forced past his blank grief for her mother, but he had arrived at Crookback Cottage a week before her child was born. He stayed with her through the birth and even after the terrible day she had to part with her baby and thought the pain would kill her.

At the time it had felt like a slender consolation for all she had lost to have her relationship with her father mended, but now it felt like the one good thing to have come out of a sad situation. If she was about to break her heart over another man Fate had made sure she couldn't have, at least she knew her father would stand by her.

'I will never wish him or Joe away, Papa, but Adam is a proud man. He has his little sister's reputation to guard and his own honour to consider. He would turn away from me in disgust if he knew what I really am.'

'What are you then, love? I know you as a passionate and impulsive girl who once loved too much rather than too little. You love with your whole heart when you love at all and if you were to fall in love again he would be a very lucky man to win you.'

'You could be biased, Papa,' she said with a rueful smile that almost wobbled into tears. But she had cried enough of them lately. 'Only think of the scandal if it ever gets out that I was an unwed mother at barely seventeen.'

'I would have lived with far worse than that to love and marry your mother,' he said with what sounded like a few unshed tears in his own voice.

She should not be surprised to see the deep sadness in his eyes as if he had only lost her mother yesterday and not twelve long, hard years ago. She had always known they loved one another beyond the usual sort of convenient aristocratic alliance, but her love with Joe had felt bigger and more generous somehow. That was the arrogance of youth, she supposed. She thought she was unique because she and Joe were so young when they stumbled into love without even having to look for it. That didn't make it less, but it did make it all the more painful when she lost him because she had expected happy ever after—life had not taught her to expect less yet so it felt like falling off the edge of the world when it happened to her so suddenly.

Loss had taught her so many painful lessons. She wondered if she could risk loving deeply and truly twice in a lifetime, but what if she didn't risk it and lost Adam anyway? Wouldn't it hurt just as much and then she would have to live with the knowledge she hadn't had the courage to fight for the might be, the lovely, undeserved triumph of love given and received once again—if she was brave enough to reach for it and maybe fail. It would be so painful to rebuild her life without another lover, without Adam.

'Losing your mother nearly sent me mad, Mel,' her father added, 'but if I had paid more attention to you and less to myself after losing her how different your life could have been.'

'I would not have it any other way, Papa. I never regretted loving Joseph or bearing his son and I never will.'

'Now I am sane again, how can I blame a dead boy for loving my wilful daughter? But perhaps you should let him lie in peace now, Mel. The last thing he would want is to see you living the half-life you slipped into after I made you give up your child.'

She couldn't say anything because he was right— she had fallen into a good enough life, first with both her grandparents, then Grandmama Granger after her grandfather died. Joseph had been too kind-hearted to have wanted her to live a lesser life because she had once loved him and borne his child in secret. She would always love and miss him and their baby, but perhaps she could hope for more from life than she had these last ten years, and that hope felt wide and joyous and horribly dangerous all at the same time.

'Forgive me?' her father said, and this time she did allow herself to cry after all.

He let his politician's aloofness drop as she sobbed against his shoulder the way she had as a child. So much loneliness and grief flowed out even she wondered when it was going to stop. 'Nothing to forgive,' she told him with a dry sob and a watery smile. 'You did your best to protect me. I'm sorry I stayed away so long.'

'So am I. Now let's tie a knot in the past and consider the future.'

'But I'm such a coward, Papa,' she whispered and felt like one as she wavered between hope and dread of what Adam might think of her if she told him the truth.

'What—my bold and headlong girl a coward? Never.'

'What if he hates me?'

'Then you will know he didn't deserve you in the first place. I think, even if he recoils from the facts at first, he will soon recall how unique and special you are and know he would be a fool to let you slip through his fingers just because you once loved another man.'

Melissa scrubbed her tears away with the handkerchief he handed her and even managed a chuckle. 'You are partisan, Papa.'

'Nonsense,' he said gruffly. 'Now, are you going to demand tea to feel better or shall we try that burgundy Berry's sent round now it's had enough time to settle?'

'Oh, definitely the burgundy,' she said. She would need some Dutch courage if she was really going to tell Adam the truth about herself.

Chapter Sixteen

'What the devil are you doing here at this time of night dressed like that?' Adam demanded as he shot out of his chair and glowered at his nocturnal visitor when she stole through the almost-secret door later that night.

'For privacy. I need to tell you something I don't want to and this was the only way I could think of to see you alone. I did load my pistol this time so there's no need to get in a temper about it.'

'What did you go to all this trouble to say to me, then?' he asked, still preoccupied with everything that could have gone wrong between here and Wiston House.

She said nothing and moved closer to the fire as if she was cold, and he finally saw tension in every line of her stiffly held body. He still had to stop his inner wolf growling hungrily when she swung the cloak off her shoulders and laid it on the nearest chair. It was enough effort to hold it back when she was dressed in dark rose silk or dove grey cambric or a domino or even guyed up like a maiden aunt.

There were always subtle hints of the fine feminine form under all those disguises, but when she was strolling about like this, slender and curvaceous and looking like no man or boy could ever look in those damned breeches of hers, it was sheer torture not to reach for her and examine those legs of hers in intimate detail, inch by silky skinned inch, until she didn't have a stitch left on. It was a fantasy he must live with until whatever had made her look so breakable was out in the open.

'What is it, my lady?' he asked more gently.

'Have you any brandy?' she said with a hitch of something that sounded like terror in her voice to say she was fighting to talk at all.

'No, I began to rely on it too much when I was first injured. I didn't want to turn into a drunkard.'

'You are too strong-willed for that,' she said, but he was glad she had never seen him at his worst, when he had been in danger of drowning in a fetid pool of resentment and self-pity. Eventually he had pulled himself out of that swamp and learnt to live with who he was instead of regretting the fool who had had the world at his feet and hadn't appreciated his luck until it ran out.

'You overestimate me, Melissa, but I did finally wean myself off the stuff, so there is claret or hock in the decanters if you really need a drink before you can say whatever you came here to say.' He tried to be light-hearted and encouraging, but his heart was beating fast with hope she was going to tell him her secrets at last. If she trusted him enough to let him know something she held so close, what did that say about her feelings for him? Hope was a dizzying emotion when you were hoping for so much, he decided as he watched her pale face and tried not to let it gallop away with him.

'I'm afraid I do,' she told him huskily, and he knew he was right. This *was* what he had been waiting to hear practically since the first moment they had met in this very room, in the nearly darkness he had been sitting here brooding in tonight instead of reading or writing letters or doing anything but dream of her and long for things he couldn't have. Yet here she was, and he was almost as nervous as she looked as she crouched in front of the fire and fed it another log to put off telling him for a few seconds longer.

'Which is it to be, then?' he asked as gently as possible with all this wild optimism to hold back with every iota of patience he could summon.

'Which what?'

'Oh, dear, even after all those years as your grandmother's scribe the English language isn't always your strong subject,' he told the top of her bright head with a wry, tender smile as she bent even further over the fire to stare into it as if it might provide answers he could not. 'Hock or claret?' he added patiently.

'Hock, please,' she said and sat back on her heels to wait for it so docilely he hated to see her so unlike her true self for fear of what she had screwed up her courage to say to him, and didn't she know him better than that by now?

He had seen how hard she was trying to close herself off from feeling whatever she felt for him last time they were together and suddenly knew it was impossible for him to do the same for much longer. He had hated the pretence they were nothing much to one another and had stormed off into the clear April sunshine to stamp about the less visited parts of the Park in peace.

Somehow he had to come to terms with the terrifying fact he had finally worked out what love was and it looked very far from being requited. Or maybe it was still possible, but she would never trust him enough to properly love him back. Love was certainly nothing like the sighing emotion poets and playwrights wrote about. It had hurt him to his very bones as he limped about the Park, scowling at nothing and cursing like a maniac. He had resented the fact of it, the feel of it so hard and prickly in his heart that his throat felt sore with it. He had had to rub a hand over his chest to remind himself to breathe. He'd wanted to stamp straight back up those steps to Wiston House and tell her so, except she would have run a mile.

She would probably go back to Shropshire, even if her grandparents were no longer there, or hide from him at Wiston Park or in some other place where he would not find her. So he had worn out the first terrible fact of it in the golden peace of one of the sleepiest parts of the capital and finally stamped home to lock himself in here and try his damnedest not to get roaring drunk. He had learned to breathe past it, to speak as if he was no different from the Adam who had set out that morning to try to force her into seeing that this fiery attraction between them could grow into something promising if they let it.

Then there it suddenly was, fully formed and almost unwanted, this knowledge it was too late to balance on the brink when he had already fallen. Love. Everything he hadn't had with Dorinda Merriot, everything he probably couldn't have with Lady Melissa Aldercombe, but he knew he would go on loving her anyway.

He was stuck with it, like his damaged knee and ruined face. Now that he had to try so hard to keep hope inside, he was as tense as a drawn bow, and she would never find the courage to confide in him if she sensed how fine drawn that was.

'Here,' he said, handing her one glass, then sitting down in a comfortable chair by the fireside to sip at his own and watch her averted face in the mellow light of the fire. Silence stretched into minutes while he watched her unique face and she watched the fire. He did his best to make her feel safe enough to confide in him. He longed to know, yet dreaded hearing this deep, dark secret of hers now they were so close to it.

What if she had killed someone? He might once have thought he could draw the line at loving a murderess, but now he knew it was too late to unlove her, whatever she had done. It was a line he could not draw so he had better hope it wasn't the ultimate human sin of taking another life that she was trying so hard to tell him.

He glanced at the clock and it said she had already been here a quarter of an hour and they were not much further on. 'It will be light again in another few hours at this time of year,' he said blandly. At least it made her look at him and even surprised a brief chuckle out of her before she went back to being serious again.

'I should be done before then,' she said.

'I'm not so sure,' he argued. 'It's taking you an unconscionable time to get to the point.' He tried to tease her into relaxing and getting it out of the way so they could move on to what came next—he liked that next, it could be his favourite part of being surprised in his library by mysterious women in breeches.

'You might decide to push me out and tell me never to come back.'

'I might, but I very much doubt it.'

'Well then, I came to tell you what I am searching for, Adam.'

'I thought you might have.'

'Don't make light of me.'

'Somebody has to if it's the only way to get whatever you are trying to say to me said. Why don't you just tell me and stop worrying, my Lady Mel?'

'It isn't just my secret,' she said with a wary look, as if she was still not certain she ought to confide even that much of this other person's secrets to anyone, and didn't she realise he wasn't just anyone, he was a someone who loved her? For a moment he wasn't even sure he wanted to know who she was protecting, but it involved her so he had to know for better or worse.

'As if I will shout anything you tell me from the rooftops, Melissa. I didn't broadcast your presence in my library the first night we met, or the second, or any of the others when we met, up to and including this one. Why won't you trust me not to give away this other person's secrets when I kept yours close?'

'They will always be first and last with me,' she told the fire very softly instead of him. His heart sank with dread as he did his best to hide the bleakness he felt at her statement of intent because that was what it sounded like. Apparently she already loved another man so much she would sacrifice Adam Lathbury and anyone else for his sake.

Her stubborn chin was set and her lioness eyes were fierce when she looked up and met his. He saw how much she loved this person when she watched him with shoulders braced and hands clenched into fists—as if it took her far more courage than he wanted to think about to tell him even that much truth and say someone else would always matter more than he did.

'Just tell me,' he said rather grimly. How could he name her *love* as he wanted to when she had kept that title back for someone else?

'Promise you will never tell another living soul what I am about to say, Adam?'

'Are we children?' he demanded, stung into speaking before he had properly thought through what he had to say. 'No, I am sorry. Of course we are not, and I can tell that this is a deadly serious matter for you so it must be for me. I promise not to reveal your secrets if you need to hear me say so to trust me. I do try to be an honourable man in the face of great provocation from certain people.'

'I suppose you mean me,' she said with a loud sigh, and apprehension snatched his breath away when she didn't even manage a smile. He took another sip of wine and tried to pretend to be as calm as a millpond. She might never tell him her secrets if she knew how close he was to telling her that nothing mattered if she would only love him and never mind this lover or stray husband or whoever she was still hesitating over telling him about.

'Of course I mean you. Now kindly get on with it, woman, before I drink myself under the table waiting for you to say whatever it is you came to say.'

'Very well, then. To start at the beginning, my lord, I suppose you must have heard all the rumours about me since I know they did the rounds all those years ago, when I should have made my debut in polite society and did not turn up that Season or any other.'

'I was too busy being dashing and interesting to take a great deal of notice of one less debutante to worry about being badgered to marry, but I do recall hearing one or two, yes.'

'Probably about my schoolgirl crush and silly elopement, followed by my cowardly suitor being paid off by my furious father, I expect,' she said with a shrug.

'Was it true—did you make a dash for the border and marriage over the anvil with a besotted swain?'

'No,' she said bleakly and stared so hard at her own feet he was glad she was not looking at him.

He didn't want her to know how much he had dreaded finding out she was secretly wed to some coward who left her on the wrong side of the anvil. He didn't have to offer to be her lover until his dying day and never mind a venal and absent husband, then, so what was she finding so difficult to say? He really hoped it wasn't that murder, because he thought she would find it even harder to live with that than he would on her behalf.

'What did you do, then?' he made himself ask her with a spark of apprehension behind the question in case he was about to become a fugitive from justice's lover.

She looked back at him with fear and sadness in her eyes and he simply couldn't keep this much distance between them any longer. 'Come here,' he said roughly and stood up, stretching out his hand towards her. He dreaded her rejecting his touch, but she took it and let him tug her on to rather wobbly looking feet.

'Stiff?' he asked as she wavered a little then stood upright and watchful at arm's length. 'Right, over here,' he added. If she knew how much of an effort it cost him to just speak the words, let alone keep his hands off her when she got here, she might not look so offended by his gruff orders.

'I'm not a dog.' She confirmed his reading of her slowness to follow his lead to the chaise.

'I know, but I can't hold you in an armchair and keep my mind on what you say.'

'Oh,' she said and made no objection when he pulled her down until she came to rest against his chest. She even seemed quite comfortable as his heartbeat raced like a runaway horse and he tried to hide his state of near-constant arousal when she was anywhere near him, let alone close enough for every sense he had to feel charged like lightning by wanting her not to talk at all, unless it was to say how much she wanted him back.

'What comes next?' he asked and kissed the top of her head so gently he wasn't sure whether she felt it, but at least she took a deep breath and began again.

'There was a man,' she said cautiously, turning to watch his face as if she knew it was a confession he must have suspected all along, but didn't really want to hear. 'Well, not a man really—even I have to admit he was more of a boy with hindsight.'

'Old enough to get you tangled up in something clandestine from the sound of things.'

'I think I was the one who did the tangling,' she said ruefully, and he could just imagine her at sixteen or so as all those rumours said she was when her life went awry. She must have been coltish and passionate and headlong, and how he wished he had met her then, before this boy of hers did whatever he did to her.

'And this boy?' he prompted her gently.

'He loved me and I loved him right back, even if it

would have looked like a totally unsuitable pairing for both his family and mine if they had known about it.'

'He was Romeo to your Juliet, then?'

'Not quite, but he did die so tragically young, Adam. Clearly I didn't poison myself rather than live without him in the approved Juliet fashion since I am still here and speaking to you now.'

'Good.'

'I almost wished I had when I found out I was with child by him after he died,' she went on without looking at him, as if now she had begun she might as well get the whole sad story out of the way, but she knew he was done with her.

She really had no idea how he felt about her, did she? Yes, it was a blow—a hard one that left him feeling raw at the idea of her so young and pregnant by this dead boy with no chance of a hasty marriage to the lad to save her good name and prevent her child being born without a father. He had to restrain himself from pulling her even closer, telling her it didn't matter what she had done then, because this was now and that was all that mattered and he loved her anyway. She needed to tell him the rest of her sad little tale and he probably needed to hear it.

'So, you lost the child?' he prompted her again.

'No,' she said starkly, and there were tears in her eyes as she looked back at him now and she was clearly lost in a past where he could not follow. 'No, I carried him to term and then I gave him away,' she told him in such a flat voice it said far too much about what it had cost her to part with her baby.

'Him?' he said gently to prompt her out of her sad reverie.

'My son. Joe's son—I bore him and gave him up.'

'And that is your deep, dark secret?' he asked, and relief made him sound as if he was taking this tragedy of hers far too lightly from the fierce look of reproach she shot him.

'My child is completely innocent. He didn't ask to be born to an unwed girl,' she insisted as if he was arguing otherwise.

'Of course he is. Do you visit the lad? Does he know you are really his mother?'

'No, the couple who took him as their own insisted on a complete break from me—there was never to be any contact between us since he was so like me. They thought it was too much of a risk that someone would put two and two together and make four. They wanted to protect him from everyone knowing he was born as my bastard son instead of as their dearly wanted child.'

'Cruel of them when they must have known you were so very young and still grieving for your lover, then you had to bid your child goodbye for ever as well,' he said.

He could see why she had cut herself off from the life a duke's daughter should have led at the very heart of the *haut ton* now. How could such a passionate, hurt and grieving girl giggle and chatter and pretend she was like the rest of the so-called Infantry? She had endured so much heartache to make her the exact opposite of all those foolish and unfledged girls.

'I truly believe they thought it for the best to make a clean break of it or I would never have let them have him. Goodness knows I argued against doing so before he was born. I wanted to pretend Lady Melissa Aldercombe had died so I could live a quiet life as a navy widow with a posthumous child to raise alone when my hero died during one of Nelson's great battles.

'I wrote letter after letter, pleading with my father and grandparents to find some way for me to keep my child. Grandmother and Grandfather Granger had to take that trip to the Continent I was supposed to have accompanied them on so I would acquire some polish before I made my debut. They were not here to help reason me out of some of my wilder schemes to keep my child, but I can assure you they were wild and hysterical, and my letters to them were probably very open and demanding because I wasn't in a state to even think about them ever being read by anyone else at the time.'

'So, *that's* what you're looking for,' he said, and of course she would move heaven and earth to protect her son. He should have known it wasn't for a lover's sake; his lioness had a cub so, of course, she would do whatever she had to do to protect him, even if it meant never seeing him again and breaking her heart over him in secret.

'Of course it is; if even one of those letters ever gets out only think what a sensation it would cause, Adam. Some busybody would be sure to think it their duty to hunt down my son and visit my sins on him.'

'What possessed your grandmother to keep even one letter from that time, then? She always seemed such a clear-thinking, sensible sort of female from her writings. I am astonished she could leave something so dangerous lying about for any curious reader to find.'

'So am I,' she said and shook her head as if she still could hardly believe the woman she loved so much could have been so careless.

'No, I just don't believe it,' he said, because it simply didn't make any sense.

'What? You don't think I'm telling the truth?' she said, looking pained and shocked that he thought she could make up such a tragic story, and of course she hadn't.

He tried to hide his pity for a girl left to struggle with terrible loss on her own, because he knew how hard pity was to endure when you wanted understanding and human warmth, and easy pity only set you at a bigger distance from your own kind. But no wonder she had poured her heart out in letters pleading to keep her coming child—where else could all the love and grief have gone when she had been so alone he wanted to travel back through time and stay with that lonely girl simply to let her know someone cared and would be there for her no matter what.

'Of course I do, woman—why would you lie about something so important and painful? I just don't believe your grandmother would be so careless of you or your child as to leave a letter like that about to be found by just anyone. I read her books and know her for a sensible and rational woman. She would never have left such a private letter lying about when she knew her home would revert to the Granger estate when she quit this world.'

'Then where is it?' Melissa asked sharply, sounding indignant that he thought he knew her grandparent better than she did.

Chapter Seventeen

Melissa felt puzzled and wrong-footed by his logic
and struggled to understand a new slant on the matter. Adam hadn't told her to go away and never come
back. He wasn't being cold and remote or looking
as if he could hardly wait for her to go away of her
own accord. He seemed to have expected her secret
to be a lot worse than it was; although it puzzled her
what he thought was worse than her bearing a child
out of wedlock when she should still have been in
the schoolroom.

'I think that's the mystery we now have to solve
together,' he said.

'Together?' she asked and could hardly believe her
ears. 'What do you mean?'

'Well, it's when two or more people join up to act
in concert to achieve a common end, or so I have
always been led to believe. In our case it is just us
and maybe your father since he obviously knows the
truth already.'

'You can't really want to help me find it now you know what I'm looking for.'

'Why not?'

'I am an unwed mother who gave her son away.'

'I'm sorry you had to part with him so finally. I can only imagine how that must have hurt when you had carried him at such a young age and with such bitter sorrow to endure all on your own. I refuse to sit in judgement of a girl who was too young to cope with her passion for a boy who was probably too young for its strength and fervour as well.

'Of course, if I had met you a decade ago, I would have tried every trick I could think of to cut him out, but how can I blame him for loving and wanting you when I love and want you so much now I find it hard to even remember my own name whenever we're together?'

'What, truly?' she said and could not let herself believe it. It felt as if he was handing her the world on a silver platter, and bitter experience had taught her life was simply not this easy.

'No, I do like a good lie,' he said with an impatient look. If he swore undying passion on his knees, he could not convince her better. His frown and irony were so typical of him she simply had to believe him.

'There's no need to be rude about it,' she told him even so.

'There's every need, you widgeon. Would I say I loved you if I was simply making game of you? Even as a silly young lord I knew what folly that was; I would have ended up wed to the first brainless chit who fancied wearing a baroness's coronet.'

'I certainly don't care about coronets and I definitely don't want to go to the Regent's coronation when it happens.'

'Neither do I, but I expect we will be obliged to whether we like it or not, unless you come up with an excuse for us both together, like imminent childbirth or mutual insanity.'

She had never expected to be half of a whole ever again after Joe died. Now Adam was taking it for granted she would marry him. How could she with such a secret to worry about for his sake now as well as her son's? It would only double the jeopardy and then do it again if they had children together.

'How can you possibly love me, Adam?'

'A question I have asked myself time and time again since you were so determined not to let yourself love or be loved ever again. I am monstrous, Melissa, so I suppose I can't blame you for doing everything you can to try to stop me doing it.'

'It's certainly not that.'

'Then what is it? What else can it be but my ghoulish looks and crippled body?'

'Ah, no, it's not that, my love. Don't ever believe it's you when it's all me.' She knelt up on the chaise to push him backwards and see his face better in both firelight and candlelight. He resisted the pressure for a moment, then sighed and let her put space between them. Her hands flattened against his broad chest and made enough of a gap for her to frown down at him.

'Mortifying yourself, are you?' he asked bitterly.

'By loving you back? Oh, very probably, my lord,' she said softly and challenged him to look away, to avoid her eyes and flinch as she used the very tips of her fingers to explore the marks that accident had written on his face.

'You can't just say something like that and expect me to sit here like a block, Lady Mel,' he said gruffly, but his gaze was still a little out of focus, as if it was the only way she had left him to avoid the shock he expected she would not be able to hide at seeing and feeling his scars in detail.

'I do expect it; I have told you about my deepest hurts and fears, Adam. I need to know what yours are if I am to believe you truly love me, knowing what you know about me now.'

'No, you don't,' he argued, his chin set hard as he clenched his teeth against her silent demand he give up his last shield against even her prying eyes, and she didn't want to pry, she just wanted to love all of him.

'My hurts only left me with scars on the inside, Adam, but you know all about them now,' she said, her touch wandering on his firm skin and gentle over the old wounds of the thorns and branches and tree bark he must have hit after somehow managing to wrestle his high-spirited and terrified team away from the child they were about to roll over with iron-shod hooves.

Instead he had shot himself and his best friend into the hedge and trees by the side of the road. She knew he had saved that small child so paralysed by fear he could not even move, let alone get to his unsteady feet soon enough to run from certain death. Melissa recalled the horrifying details Cousin Phillida had told her at the time and felt ashamed she had done her best to forget them until she had met him and found that old letter and read it again.

Phillida had mourned the loss of such a handsome man's looks and easy strength, but Melissa felt the pain of all he had really lost as he did his best to meet her eyes now and still hide it from her somehow. He was protecting her from the full weight of his pain as well as his grief for his friend, so it didn't feel as if he thought of her as an equal at all. Adam had saved a child's life at such a heavy cost to his own. It made her want to cry for him and rage at the Fates for being so cruel.

If she gave in to tears she knew he would retreat into his shell and defend himself against her pity, but she didn't pity him. She grieved the loss of his best friend and his old life for him, and maybe even the shattering of his old easy confidence. But his feelings mattered more than the tears she had to blink away impatiently. Adam was her hero, her love and simply his gallant, brave, stubborn self. He was nothing like this fictional monster he seemed to have decided he must be after the accident had taken so much from him. Now all she had to do was make him realise he was a better man for all of that agony and not a worse one.

'How can I love you and not love every one of these as well? They are part of you, a small piece of what made you who you are now—the man I admire and want and long to love with all my heart and live with if you will only let me,' she whispered and still felt him flinch as if her touch abraded wounds that healed long ago.

'They are part of a monster,' he said disgustedly and still avoided her gaze as she ran her fingertips over the gouged lines on his cheek and around his eyepatch. 'Don't ask it of me, Mel,' he said hoarsely as she stopped her touch just short of the black patch and waited patiently for him to let her further into his secret self, as she had let him into hers.

'I am not asking, my lord, I'm demanding,' she told him with a queenly look. She waited with her heart beating at the gallop to be accepted or rebuffed. If he could not let her into his very private self, there could be no future for them together.

'Very well,' he gritted out between clenched teeth. 'Do it,' he said tightly and leaned back against the damask upholstery as if it took too much strength to hold his head up while he waited for her to see what she guessed nobody else had seen clearly since his last doctor left, after telling him there was no more they could do for His Lordship's sight in his damaged eye.

'Very well,' she echoed his words with a wicked smile. 'I will,' she whispered, 'but first…' She let her voice tail off because there were much better things to do with her mouth than talking. Instead of using her fingertips she bent her head and kissed the corner of his mouth where the scars began and explored them in such rich detail she almost forgot why she ever started this and got distracted from her purpose of showing him he was her absolute pleasure to kiss and explore and never mind the marks of his accident on his face and body.

She wanted all of him, every bit of him that was scarred or perfect, seeing or unseeing. She heard his breath hitch, but even under the onslaught of what she knew was a very mutual desire the tension did not quite leave his rigid body as she knelt over him, enjoying the touch and taste of intimacy, the feel of his skin against her lips, showing him how much more there was to know than he thought and how dearly she wanted every inch.

'There's no need for you to mortify yourself to prove a point,' he told her curtly, as if he was forcing the words out to defend himself when she got to the worst of him and decided she didn't want to know him any better after all.

'Idiot,' she raised her mouth long enough to murmur softly, and she looked down at him with all she felt in her eyes, or at least she hoped so. Whatever he saw in her face his visible eye told her good things about. It went velvet dark with desire and heady emotions she could not let them explore fully quite yet.

They would get carried away and she knew he was secretly hoping that they would and she would forget all about this last secret left between them. She was so tempted to sink her mouth on his and forget the rest in loving him in every sense. *No*, this was too important to be forgotten in a frantic coupling.

'Later,' she promised them both as she went back to knowing him as no other woman had ever done before. If he had taken lovers since his accident, she knew he would not have let them do this. He would not uncover his damaged eye even in the throes of passion. She tried not to be jealous of the women who had shared his bed before her, even if they would never know the secret all of him she was about to learn.

Hard to keep her goal in mind while she was seducing him, inch by slow inch, and it was so utterly pleasurable to have the freedom to know him this intimately. Yet she was a determined woman and resisted the ultimate temptation. It took all the willpower she had as she waited at the edge of his eyepatch for his last concession and held her breath.

'Get it over with, woman,' he demanded hoarsely, as if he was too near the end of his tether to say anything more.

'Very well,' she whispered and felt among his sooty curls for the string of his eyepatch. She had to spare his glossy raven locks a caress or two while she was round there before she found the bow and tugged at it. He felt so tense under her exploring fingers she wondered if she had hurt him, but from the rigid strain in every muscle of his body this was far more serious than a few pulled hairs for him. At last she lifted the patch away and took her first look at the damaged eye he had done everything he could to hide from her.

'Well, I can't really see what all the fuss is about,'

she said as the scarring at one side of his eye and the whiteness over about half of his eyeball struck her as a pity, but nothing she could ever find ugly or be fearful of seeing as his fondest lover yet.

'What? You don't find it repulsive?' he asked as if he thought she couldn't have looked at it hard enough.

'No, I wish you could see with it and even more that the accident had never happened and left you so badly hurt in body and mind, but that's all there is to worry me about it. There is certainly nothing I will ever feel squeamish about if that's what bothers you. It looks like a storm in a teacup to me.'

'A...?' he began to echo her, but words failed him. He pushed her gently away, seized the candelabra from his desk and strode over to the mirror with it as if he must check that he hadn't turned into a prince since the last time he looked in one.

'Well?' she demanded, her hands on her hips as he left her in a ridiculous position, kneeling up like an abandoned hound begging for attention.

'Well what?'

'What do you see?'

'A ruin, a wreck—the shadow of the man I used to be.'

'Then you are vain,' she told him, getting off the chaise to stroll over and join him.

'Vain?' he spat indignantly as if the very word was poison to him. 'How can that *thing* ever be vain?' he demanded with a contemptuous wave at his face in the mirror as if he hated it.

'You might not be as pretty as you used to be,

Lord Lathbury, but you are clearly not satisfied with being handsome enough. That looks like vanity from where I'm standing.'

'Then you're not standing close enough.'

'I am now,' she told him as she insinuated herself under the arm he had stretched out to wave at his reflection in the mirror and demand she saw him as he saw himself. 'Vanity, vanity, all is vanity,' she teased him as her reflection joined his in the mirror, and how else was she ever going to get through to him she loved him, scars and all? And how could she *not* love them when they were simply one more part of who he was?

'Belle fainted the first time she saw me after the accident,' he said hoarsely and as if it still hurt him to recall his little sister's horrified reaction when she saw the damage to his face and body when he was healed just enough to see her. Melissa supposed that experience set him on the road to thinking himself hideous even before his fiancée jilted him. Then all those silly girls flinched away from him the other night and carried on the bad work.

'How old was your sister five years ago?'

'Thirteen.'

'Still a child, then. I expect she had been worrying herself to a shadow about you all the time you were ill and everyone feared for your life as well. She must have been so terribly afraid that she was going to lose you, the poor child.'

'You could be right,' he admitted and raised his

hand to his face as if he might want to become better acquainted with it after all.

'Could be? Of course I am. Can you see anything with that eye?' The wild hope she had struggled against since she first met him was joined by a new tenderness, and maybe he did need her almost as much as she did him.

'The difference between light and dark, perhaps?' he said with a frown as if he was wondering at himself now he had taken the eyepatch off and the world had not fallen apart. 'I don't often give it a chance to find out.'

'No, I wager you put on your eyepatch the instant you wake up, even before your valet has a chance to catch you without it.'

'I do, but I could make an exception for my wife,' he told her and gave her a wildcat grin that gave her an idea of the eligible, desirable and very sure of himself Lord Lathbury of five years ago, before tragedy had made him into the one she loved so much now.

'Best make sure it's only for her, then,' she said jealously.

'Only if she is you, Melissa; I couldn't do it for whatever perfect female you are busily making up in your head for me to wed instead of you at this very moment. I shall never have or even want a wife if I can't have you.'

'You really do love me, then? Even knowing what I did?'

'Of course I do—why wouldn't I?'

'Because I bore another man's child out of wedlock

and have sincerely mourned him for over a decade,' she said starkly. She was the one who could not quite believe he had taken in the full weight of her disadvantages this time.

'Can you put him behind you just enough to leave room to love me as well?' he asked as if he still expected her to weigh up the yeas and nays and end up with no.

'Of course I can. I was a heedless, headstrong girl back then. Now I am a woman, love feels so different I cannot even compare it and I don't want to. I'm not sure I would have loved the vain and entitled Lord Lathbury you were then half as much as I do you, though.'

'Yet I would have envied your young lover his impulsive, untamed Lady Melissa if we had met then, so it's probably just as well we did not.'

'And I did truly love him, Adam, I can't lie that it was a girlish crush because I know Joseph would have grown into a good man if only he had been given the chance.'

'Of course he would; you loved him,' he said as if it was that simple, and she felt something painful break inside her.

She had held herself so stiff and cold for so many years it felt as if Adam's warmth was dragging the needy, loving and wildly impulsive Melissa of all those years ago across to join the one he loved now. The wonder of it made her feel shaky and exposed at the same time as she was free and warm and hopeful again. He had just made himself vulnerable to her by letting her see his damaged eye, and it felt as if he was seeing the worst of her as well and showing her the past was all part of what made her who she was now. Even then she had to test out his tolerance as he had done when he was staring in that mirror, exploring the man she saw instead of the monster he had made himself into.

'My lover was a farmer's son, Adam. One of the best and most prosperous farmers on my father's primary estate, but if you are going to find him less because he was born in a farmhouse you had better do it now and know exactly who and what my Joseph was before we two go any further.'

'I have learned to see good and bad in all walks of life by now, Melissa. Maybe it took this to humble me and drive that truth home, but I learned in the end,' he said with an almost casual wave at his scarred face.

But she knew this was still a big leap for such a proud man. She had loved another man before him and that made it one for her as well. She was still desperate to keep her son's existence a secret from the rest of the world and the threat of that letter jarred through her once again. She shivered with apprehension and thought of what it could do to their lives if they were wed when someone else found it and told the world, but if Adam was brave enough to risk it she supposed she had to be brave enough to let him.

'And don't forget you're a duke's daughter and I'm just a humble baron,' he said with a cocky smile that argued he wasn't humble at all. Perhaps he was reminding her there was joy and laughter as well as risk in loving one another wholeheartedly, and perhaps he was right. But, oh, dear, that risk felt perilous with that letter her grandmother was so worried about as she lay dying still not found and safely destroyed.

'You don't seem very humble to me, but are you sure, Adam?'

'Of course I am, woman; do you expect me to go down on my knees and beg?'

'Not on those poor old knees you have to limp about on so painfully,' she told him with a wicked smile as her see-sawing emotions almost made her believe love would prevail because he loved her so much how could it not?

'Baggage,' he told her with that dear, wry smile of his. 'Marry me anyway?'

'Yes, as long as we find that letter.'

'No ifs and caveats, Melissa. Don't make it a condition because I cannot and will not live with half-measures.'

'How can we marry with the threat of exposure still hanging over me?'

'If you care so much what other people think, then you cannot truly love me, Melissa,' he said shortly. 'And I don't care what the polite world says about you or me.'

'I love you too much to stand by while you fight duels with sneering dandies because of me. I could not bear it if you were to shut yourself up in this library even more often than you already do to avoid hearing what the wider world are whispering about me either, so don't bother to promise you would never see enough of them to fight for my honour because that really doesn't make me feel any better.'

'Then you don't love me enough to take a risk and marry me anyway. You took plenty for your first love, though, didn't you, Melissa?'

'That's not the point; I love you enough to walk away from you rather than see you and yours hurting because you married me and cannot disown a scandal I wilfully brought into your family when I said yes to you. I have my pride as well, Adam. I hate the very idea of you being thought less of because of me, and I did bear a bastard in secret and gave my baby away to hide my disgrace and pretend nothing much happened.'

'No! That's not who you are or what you did. Stop making me into a noble sacrifice and see sense for once in your stubborn life. I love you. I never want to live without you at the centre of my life and causing mayhem and magic wherever we go. Damn it, woman, I love *you* and just you until my dying day. Either love me back truly and passionately and accept everything we are and can be together or go away and leave me to be lonely and loveless and not quite happy for the rest of my life without you in it. I would rather have even that than just half your heart and a head full of ifs and maybes.'

Faced with the stark idea of her life without him, she simply could not do it any longer. Maybe it was little and cowardly of her, but the thought of missing him with every breath she took for the rest of her life felt so grievous she couldn't endure it. 'I do love you, Adam, but don't blame me if this whole scandal blows up in our faces one day.'

'Idiot,' he said and kissed her long and deep and hungrily.

'Take me to bed, then,' she whispered shakily when they finally had to take a breath.

'You're not getting yourself with child out of wedlock a second time.'

'I didn't do it entirely by myself last time,' she said, and her heart beat heavily and refused to quiet down again as his mouth set stubbornly.

'Don't remind me,' he growled as if he was jealous of her first lover however hard he tried not to be.

'You had better marry me next week, then,' she teased him as desire made her want everything he was so determined not to let them have, and even a week felt like for ever to wait for some delicious, wondrous relief from it and then there was fulfilment and more... Best not think about that more when he wanted it to be so far off.

He looked thoughtful for a moment and nodded when she was only joking. 'If not sooner,' he said.

'It's already Tuesday,' she replied with her heart racing at the very idea. 'We can't, Adam,' she objected because she had to, despite all the fierce love and wanting she could be revelling in until they were speechless and boneless and beyond thought right now, if he didn't have a will of iron and a gallant determination their first child would not arrive even a day before it ought to. Which reminded her it would not be her first one and she still had her son to consider. 'And I still have to find that letter.'

He turned away from her, left her staggering on feet that felt as if they didn't belong to her so he could pace his library again, his limp more pronounced as his pent-up fury became starkly obvious. She knew she had hurt him again.

'*We* have to find it,' he barked when he came back to her.

She was afraid someone would hear him through the door and come to find out what he was grumbling about to himself in here. A fine to-do that would cause with her in breeches and him so furious he would not care who saw her. 'Whatever we do, stop shouting.'

'Aye,' he said, running a hand through his already ruffled hair. She wanted to say anything, do anything he wanted simply because he wanted it. 'I'm sorry,' he added gruffly. 'I want to matter more than they do, but I know this is about your son.'

'Always, none of it is his fault.'

'None of it is anyone's fault. Like this,' he said with an impatient wave at his scarred face. 'It was just an accident.' Had he accepted a terrible mischance made that child escape his mother's vigilance and run into the path of Lord Lathbury's racing curricle at exactly the wrong moment at last, then?

'It was certainly an accident when Joe fell off that roof in the rain, but our baby wasn't one,' she admitted reluctantly because she still wanted him to think the best of her. 'I was set on marrying him, whatever his parents or my father would say about the inequality of our birth, and I didn't intend to wait five years until I was of age and could marry without their consent.

'Our baby was quite deliberate on my part and Joe never could hold out against me when I wanted something badly enough. I wanted his child so much I would have done anything to get on with having one to make us a family. He could not have known I was with child when he climbed that roof, but he did know we did a great deal of loving in order to make one,' she admitted and finally let herself be angry with her dead love for taking that risk anyway.

At the time grief for his promise and all her love and the friend she had lost as well sucked the fury out of her, but how she would have let it fly if only he had survived that stupid risk he only took to prove what a man he was to his father's farmhands. 'And he went up there anyway,' she admitted at last. 'And because he did, I must still find that letter.'

'Not alone.'

'No, not alone any more,' she said, and it felt, well, it was beyond words how she felt, but not beyond actions.

Chapter Eighteen

'A week isn't very long,' she murmured and brushed against his muscular body with as much wicked intent as she could fit into one incendiary gesture.

'It will feel hellish enough without you making it worse,' he told her brusquely and did his best to push her away without hurting her.

'No, it will be just long enough to show you how much I adore having you as my pirate lover,' she said because she had recently discovered she had as much headlong passion in her as there was in the old days with some more added on for maturity and, loving him so much, she wasn't prepared to wait another day, let alone a whole week.

'I can't endure the idea of me leaving you alone with my child in your belly and no wedding ring on your finger, my Melissa,' he told her as if the very thought of it hurt.

She wrapped herself a little bit closer until she felt the mighty frustration in his trembling body and knew she wasn't going to wait even so. How could they wait with all this fire and passion and pent-up emotion driving her half-mad? Goodness knew what it was doing to him, and she let herself feel the rigid fact of his erection against her body and wriggled a little closer to appreciate it properly, or maybe even improperly, she supposed with a purr of satisfaction and glorious anticipation.

'Then make sure you stay alive,' she demanded. 'In fact, you can do that every day for the next fifty years or more since I refuse to even think about living without you ever again.'

'You're sure?' he said, his deep voice so husky with desire she told herself she was having to rise on tiptoes and get closer to his mouth simply to hear him.

'Do I feel unsure?' she asked just as softly as she pressed her body even closer until her unencumbered legs were wound close to his and his mighty arousal was hard against her hot and needy core. 'I think I will melt from unfulfilled desire if you don't love me as completely and immoderately as I need to love you, Adam.'

'And we can't have that,' he whispered.

'What if your grandmother and sister come home unexpectedly again?' she had just enough sense left to mutter as he found her nipples desperate for him and rubbed his palms over her needy breasts until she moaned with desperation.

'In here,' he said as if he could only just manage those words before he lost the power of speech. They were inside the dark little chamber his librarian would be shocked to know harboured his employer and a scandalous lady so busy tumbling into love in every sense of the word.

Melissa almost laughed when Adam found just enough presence of mind to shut the door behind them and lock them in. She wondered what anyone who lingered long enough to hear them would make of the odd little lovers' noises coming from this almost a cupboard. Then she was so wound up in making love with him she forgot the rest of the world.

Dusty darkness only made them more intimate as he shielded her from the hard wood of the table by sitting on it himself and pulling her into his body with a groan of heated desire that made her heart beat even faster and excitement open up inside her, and didn't that feel glorious, and alive and *oh, yes*, but she was desperate for more. She was free to be who she truly was again at long last. Free to be wild, headlong Melissa, who loved without boundaries and lived so fiercely in the moment he had given her back a part of herself she had been so ashamed of for far too long.

'I need you so much, Adam,' she told him and kissed him greedily. She was so impatient to get her breeches off and love him fully her hands were too unsteady and hurried to do it herself, so he did it for her. He actually knelt at her feet to undo shoelaces and stockings and buckles with shaking fingers so when he stood up again her breeches fell round her ankles and she kicked them impatiently away. By then she was silenced by a fearsome need to be with him in every way there was. She smoothed herself against him like hot silk, her body stretched against his.

He was half sitting on that convenient table again, but this time there was nothing between her and him, and his kiss was hot and urgent and heady on her open mouth, his hands deliciously firm on her wanting breasts as they bowed together, and then he was inside her in one smooth, powerful movement. He stilled with her held above him, half kneeling, half held in his mighty arms, and they were joined so intimately together as she took in the full wonder of being loved by Adam Lathbury with every last inch of his manhood high inside her. She felt the wide, inviting pleasure of being filled and driven and wanting like this with him for the first time.

She flexed experimentally on his mighty member and it jerked inside her as if it had an independent will of its own and was driving him mad as well as her. He muffled a groan in the tender place between her shoulder and her throat and licked her hammering pulse as she rocked upwards to feel the delicious friction she was so desperate for now, and he encouraged her to set their pace with his supporting hands. It felt so urgent and tender in here with him in the dark she had to make it a race after all, because she was in danger of bursting into ecstasy long before he did if she didn't hurry them on faster than he thought was quite gentlemanly to go when this was her first time in for ever.

She felt so hot, so light and sure and so good at this she stretched her arms above her head and gloried in the power they could share between them. She gasped with exquisite pleasure when he took one of her nipples in his mouth and suckled on her. If she wasn't already driven and gasping and frantic for even more before, she would be now. She felt her cheeks flush and even her breasts were hot and blushing although he couldn't see them, but he must have known how needy they were since he cupped one, and the delicate stroke of his fingers on her aching nipples felt like fire and the sweetest pleasure.

There was yet another layer of intimacy as he murmured heady praise before his mouth seized hers again and his tongue danced explicitly with hers to shadow the driven rhythm of their bodies. They were suspended on the very edge of wonder for an endless, driven moment until he thrust upwards even as she clenched around him and drove downwards so they pulsed into driven fulfilment together. Wrapped around one another in the heavy darkness spasms of the most intense pleasure she had ever known drove through her until it felt like flying or dreaming or just being so close to the man she loved it was absolute pleasure and completeness and joy. She felt his climax even as she lost herself in them, spinning together into driven spasms of ecstasy. It felt as if they had joined everything they were to make a new world only they could visit.

They went on kissing and stroking and praising one another with incoherent murmured words as joyous aftershocks kept them locked intimately together, and this dark little room felt like infinite space. She was languid with loving, and warm and wonderfully smug about it as they drifted back to it being a midnight tryst in my lord's fine library with Lady Melissa Aldercombe being wicked and wanton and where nobody would ever expect her to be, but here she still was, and very delightful and delicious it was, too.

'Well, at least that's the last of the fuss and formality over and done with for today,' Adam said with a very satisfied grin a week later. 'It took a whole week to accomplish, but at least you were worth the wait, my lady.'

'Was I now?' Melissa said, knowing he was making a game of their quiet wedding for her sake.

'Definitely, although I must say that a special licence is shockingly expensive.'

'The wider world will call it a hole-and-corner affair when they find out about it.'

'Not in front of my grandmother or your father they won't.'

'Or you.'

'Oh, I won't be listening. I shall be far too busy adoring my expensive new wife to listen to idle gossip.'

'You might have to if...' she began to say, but he didn't let her finish. He kissed her with such pent-up hunger she almost believed in that endless week of his after all.

It was fire in the veins, thunder in her heart, and she wanted him again so badly that she ached and longed and yearned for him as if they had never made love wherever they could make space and time and darkness enough not to be discovered doing it this last week. His wicked mouth and roving hands let her know how urgently he wanted her, and her inner wanton purred and stretched and yearned for him right back. 'We can't, Adam, not in a coach.'

'Your horizons clearly need expanding, Lady Lathbury,' he said with another wicked smile to invite her to think about all the delicious possibilities for amorous adventures with a very willing husband. 'Although we had better save your re-education for another time, since I see we are about to arrive at our destination.'

'Are we? That didn't take long.'

'Or maybe I am just very good at kissing my new wife.'

'Maybe you are, Husband,' she said, and the wonder of today sank in now the irresistible, incredible fact of him loving her overtopped the nerves and qualms. She was married! 'I never thought I would have one of those weddings, Adam,' she said shakily. 'I thought I must walk alone for the rest of my life.'

'And I thought I must limp alone through mine, my darling,' he joked because he knew all about those nerves and doubts of hers, and she loved him all the more for trying to make the fuss of even such a small wedding easier on her. 'How on earth will I get through the next few hours without seizing my brand-new wife and carrying you off to my lair for our mutual pleasure, my siren Lady Melissa?'

'I love you so much, Adam,' she said, 'but with

your grandmother and my father so determined to celebrate even very quietly we must behave ourselves for once.'

'I don't see why,' he said and didn't even wait until the footmen jumped down and pulled down the step for her to alight from his fine carriage before lifting her into his arms. They were up the steps to his town mansion before she could protest about his knees and her weight and all the other reasons a wife had to worry about her husband.

'Stop fussing and save your breath, my lovely,' he told her as he set her on her feet again with a rueful look at the stairs to admit they might be a little too much to carry her all the way up and still be able to perform his lordly duties when they got to that master suite she had fantasised over so wistfully when they first met.

'What about our wedding breakfast?' she gasped as she let him tug her up those stairs.

'We'll have it in bed,' he told her as they scurried along the wide corridor towards wedded bliss, at long last. 'It's been two days and I'm too hungry for my Lady Lathbury to even think about food.'

'I do like a nice shadowy library,' Melissa said breathlessly after she and Adam had joyously celebrated the anniversary of being my lord and lady for a week now in their own very particular style.

'Now what I like is my wife inside one with me and a locked door at our backs. You should also be wearing very little or nothing at all, my beauty,'

Adam said with a piratical leer at her sitting naked in front of the fire they had decided they would need even this late in the spring, since they would be wearing little or nothing at all.

She laughed, still rather breathless as they had been enjoying being in this one so thoroughly it was going to take some time for her to get her breath back. All the wild and impossible fantasies she thought would never come true during the first days of their short and unusual courtship could be played out now. After the latest one had come true she was warm and wondering and felt seduced to her fingertips.

She smiled at him without even bothering to hide her enchantment with her husband and all the wondrous things they could do to one another now they were safely wed. All the things she never thought she would have, she recalled with a little hiccup in her delight at being my Lady Lathbury, she hastily thrust to the back of her mind so she could concentrate on her own personal lord properly once again.

'I do love you, Adam,' she told him as he reached for the fine Kashmir shawl they had tossed on the chaise however long ago it was since they hastily disposed of it and the rest of her clothes, wherever *they* might be. He tucked the beautiful silky thing around her before settling down next to her on the rug by the fire. 'I might boil,' she said with a wry smile.

'We can undo you again later, love, but for now just indulge me,' he said and moved so he could curl his big body around hers so they were skin-to-skin, spooned lovers who were almost spent. Only almost, she realised with a wicked smile as she felt his already half-aroused sex against her and laughed softly at his endless desire for his wife, even after the banquet for the senses they had just served one another and all the others they had managed to fit into the last week of wedded bliss and the heady week of unwed bliss they enjoyed so immoderately before that.

'You're a disgrace, my lord,' she murmured with sleepy sensuality.

'I am, my lady,' he said, 'but luckily I met my match in you.'

'I was always a disgrace. You were the one who took all the risks by marrying me,' she said half seriously, and that misstep in her joy and happiness at finding him and all these wonders shot a tension through her she didn't even know she felt until he wrapped her even closer and sat them both upright so she was surrounded by warmth and masculinity and his deep and abiding love.

'The only risk was you would never let us love like this, my Lady Mel,' he whispered huskily in her nearest ear. 'That was the possibility I was terrified of every night on from the one when we first met until you were safely married to me. Now I have all the fire and glory I never even realised I wanted so much in my lordly, lonely bed until the night I met you.'

'And now I have been that wife on your lordly desk and your lordly chaise and all the other places my inventive lord can be lordly and potent and my lover on or in without quite managing to scandalise your entire staff and all your curious neighbours.'

'Our staff, our neighbours,' he corrected her with a frown she reached up to smooth away with a loving touch that threatened to get a lot more loving, until he took her hand and kissed it solemnly then held both of hers in his and wrapped them across her belly to stop them roaming.

'You will have to get used to being part of me and the other half of my life, Melissa,' he said a little bit too seriously when the fire and excitement she always felt as a delicious undercurrent nowadays whenever he was near beckoned and promised, although she thought it was all but impossible for there to be any more only a few short minutes ago as ecstasy shook through them like…well like itself, she decided. She eyed the fire dreamily and tried to come up with words for this love and delight and mutual joy that went way beyond the power of them.

'I love you, Adam. I am just not so sure I can ever love being part of the *ton* or running a great house like this one or all the other houses you seem to have waiting for me to try to be mistress of.'

'It's all a part of me; I can't shrug it off and pretend none of it exists, Mel.'

'No, of course you can't, and I wouldn't want you to. It's just…' She let the words fade away again because they felt inadequate for very different reasons this time.

'Just that you cannot forget the hubris you think is always hiding behind the joy of us finding one another against the odds and waiting to pounce on it and destroy us,' he said very seriously. He was right and he was also far better with these dratted words than she was.

'No, I can't. I'm sorry,' she admitted with a heavy sigh and drew up her knees so she could rest her chin on them and still have his arms strong about her waist and his mighty body all around her. 'Does that position hurt you?' she whispered as the feel of his muscles and satin skin behind her was the comfort and joy she needed, but what about him?

'No, but you'd best not wriggle too much or something else will hurt a great deal more than my weak knee or any of the other weaknesses I suffer from.'

'They aren't weaknesses, they're strengths,' she argued fiercely.

'You can say that to me even as you refuse to value your own formidable strengths? What a contrary, aloof lady that does make you, Lady Lathbury.'

She stared at the fire and thought through his half accusation and half praise. 'I expect you're right,' she said and twisted round to stare up at him for a moment, then grew tired of the effort it cost her straining muscles. Scrambling her body around carefully enough not to hurt him, she knelt up to stare into his eyes and tried to show him all she felt and wanted to feel for him. 'I don't want to be aloof with you, Adam,' she told him seriously, even if it was from the least aloof position she could think of and while almost in a state of nature with her beloved, passionate husband.

'But the contrary part is perfectly all right?' he murmured, then shook his head. 'No, you're right, my Melissa, this is serious. We need to deal with it once and for all, before it makes us less than we ought to be together.'

'I don't see how. We have searched every trivial note and every page of my grandmother's extensive collection of books twice over now and found no trace of that letter she wrote so painfully about almost with her last breath.'

'Was she confused and incapable after the apoplexy?'

'She was incapacitated, but I could see from her eyes and the sounds and gestures she could make how frustrated she was at not being able to say what she wanted to.'

'There must actually be a letter, then. The fact she managed to write about it at all argues she was trying to leave you a clue where it is. Maybe we just have to reason our way through every possibility until we find the right one.'

'Do you think I haven't tried to do that time and time again?' she said with bitter frustration for all the hours they had spent going through her grandmother's books and papers to be sure she hadn't missed some cunningly cut binding or written-in-the-margins clue.

'You might be too close to see it properly. Come on,' he said, rising to his feet with only a slight hesitancy in his lithe movements, and she wondered if loving as strongly as they did now had taken some of his self-consciousness about his limp away.

Maybe it would physically lessen now he was not thinking about it and feeling bitterly self-conscious, for how could he do that when she lusted after his powerful masculine body so voraciously he had to know it was truly magnificent by now.

'Come on, lazybones,' he said and tugged her on to her feet and tucked her shawl round her more securely before she could dwell on her husband's physical perfections and forget her quest again. 'We need to concentrate,' he told her with mock severity as she made a face at him for bundling her up in her shawl like an infant after its bath and did her best to forget how much she wanted to simply love him over and over again and never mind anything else.

'Thinking about it whenever I'm not preoccupied with you hasn't done me any good up to now,' she argued sulkily as he led her over to the desk and pulled out the chair she had been sitting in the first time she ever laid eyes on him. 'I'm so glad I broke into your library one dark night all those weeks ago, my lord,' she said dreamily as she sat down with the sensuous feel of finest cloth against her bare skin.

The Lady Melissa who had come in here so self-sufficient and alone that night and this one, all but naked in her husband's private lair and deeply happy about it, were so different it made her realise how wondrous the complete change in her life from then to now truly was.

'So am I. Now stop trying to divert me, woman, and write down exactly the same words as your grandmother wrote, in exactly the same order, so we can get this business sorted out and get back to enjoying ourselves immoderately again in peace.'

'No, I can't. I can't write it down. I dare not,' she said in a fine panic, as if the busiest of busybodies might be hiding in the shadowy corners of the room and see the words that had linked up so disastrously in her head the first time she read them. She felt the panicky certainty nothing about her life would ever be safe again. Unless she could get that letter back she would be sucked her into her worst nightmares.

'We have a fire, Mel, so stop panicking like a frightened hen with a fox on her tail and just hurry up and write it out for me. As soon as I read it we can burn it and nobody else will ever see it, but I need to know exactly what she wrote to you.'

'Very well,' Melissa said with a great sigh and set herself to recall exactly what her grandmother wrote with such a painful effort. She thought hard and crossed one word out and substituted another for strict accuracy, then she showed it to Adam.

'Melissa, find, letter, mother, and son, with, my book,' he read out, and she wanted to hush him in case someone could hear them here—in the middle of a large locked room, in the middle of the night. He was right, wasn't he? She was far too tense and much too close to this to tell sense from nonsense in her own mind, let alone her grandmother's dying words.

'You could say your son has two mothers,' Adam said after staring down at the words she had written out from memory with a thoughtful frown on his face for several minutes of tense silence, while she tried to reason her way through her own terror and out the other side. Thank goodness he was being rational because all these weeks of worry and tension and falling in love with him so suddenly and unexpectedly must have softened her brain.

'I suppose so,' she said, her old reluctance to name the woman who held her child's happiness in her hands his mother, when she had wanted to be his true one in every way there was so badly that it still hurt.

'Even if she told you all ties were to be broken between you and your child, do you think your grandmother would so as well? His mother might even want a way left open herself in case anything ever happened to her and her husband,' he said gently, as if he thought she might fire up at him for even thinking he knew her grandmother better than her.

She sat silent for a while and let his revolutionary view of her son's adoption sink in, then felt a complete fool. 'I must be very slow, or simple,' she said at last. She was angry with herself for never thinking this through logically. 'Of course, my grandmother must have known far more than she pretended to about a couple so desperate for a child they were happy to call my baby their own. She would never have put her great-grandson in the hands of people she didn't know and trust, and why did I never realise it before, Adam?'

'Because you were distraught and empty and grieving for your lover and your child,' he said as if he wanted to go back to that time and offer her comfort.

She was glad he could not because she would have rejected it. She had refused to talk to her grandparents or her father about what had happened to her and wrapped it all inside her until she had made a

hard shell around her heart that took ten years, another lot of grief and damaged, unique Adam Lathbury to break and show her it was safe to love again,
but only with him.

'And if you knew where and who and how your
boy is, could you leave him there to be who he thinks
he is if he is safe and content, my Mel?' he asked her
gently now, and it didn't seem quite fair that he knew
her better than she knew herself.

She had already opened her mouth to say *Of
course I could* before she realised that was a lie and
shut it again. It would be the ultimate in temptation
to see for herself if her son was well and happy and
still as like her as a pea in a pod. She made herself
meet Adam's steady gaze and see all the reservations
he had about picking up the clue she missed and following it to its logical conclusion.

'I can now,' she said at last and felt the strength of
that decision flow through her and burn out some of
the bitter sorrow of having had to part with her baby
when she was not much more than a child herself. 'I
couldn't have done it ten years ago and doubt I could
have now until I met you,' she told him with every
ounce of sincerity she had in her, because it was true.
'But I can now.'

'Then maybe your grandmother was right to hold
their secret for you as she did.'

'Yes, I suppose she was, but she kept it too well. If
my father had any idea about it, we would have been
saved so much worry.'

'And we would never have met.'

'Oh, no, that's a terrible idea!' she said and felt as if the earth might drop away from under her feet at such a horrible idea and leave her so alone again without him. 'I can't even think about how empty my life would be without you, Adam,' she whispered and put her hand over her mouth to keep it from wobbling at the awfulness of that notion.

'I was so lonely without you for so long,' she added, and she knew how true it was now and how richly her life had changed since she let herself into his library that first night, so intent on finding a very different letter from the one this one could turn out to be, if she ever found it.

'I think Fate must have been on our side all along, then,' he said with his wry, self-deprecating smile and all the love she could hardly believe her luck about in his dark velvet gaze. Better call it velvet and silver for his damaged eye, she corrected herself as she gazed back at him, entranced by every detail of her warrior lover, who only ever left that last guard off with her, his wife. 'Living without you was bitter,' he added huskily.

'Don't call it Fate, love. I railed at it so hard let's not tempt it. Call it a lifetime of luck if you like, but let's not give that fickle monster any more power over us.'

'Let's get back to our sheep and track them down while we can still think about something other than one another, then. We haven't quite got down the list of all the ways I want you that we didn't discuss prop-

erly on our second night in this room, when I let you
know I want you any way I can get you, my lady.'

'And you expect me to be able to think at all after
you have reminded me of it?'

'I expect you to be exceptional, as you always are,'
he said, and she sat a little straighter in his chair and
stared at the page in front of her because he thought
she could, and all of a sudden it made sense after all.

'Her book, Adam!' she exclaimed and felt a complete fool and not in the least bit exceptional as she
gazed down at the words she had written, then back
up at him, and of course that was where it would be.

'We looked in every one of the ones she had pub-
lished during her lifetime and every single note and
reference she made, and you wrote down for her before
she was incapacitated and could write no more books,
just in case we missed something significant. You
know we could not miss anything when we looked
through them all separately and together.'

'But think, love—there are other books all of us
call our own and not just the writers who actually
write them.'

He stared at her, then looked around the room as
if one of his books might give him a clue to what she
was talking about.

'Not you perhaps, you probably have far too many
of them to single out just one,' she teased him, and it
felt so freeing and right to be able to joke about this
at last that she almost bounced out of her chair and
hugged him. She saw his eyes go hot and avid again
as her breasts jiggled with her hasty movements and

the shawl hung disregarded over her shoulders to give him a very good view of all of Lady Lathbury stark naked underneath it.

'Not now,' she said and hastily covered herself up again. 'Soon, but not right now,' she added as this constant current of sensual awareness argued why not, as well as his reproachful look and very obvious arousal.

'I would give up every page in here for a single night with you, love,' he murmured and cleared his throat and looked away as if that was the only way he could think about anything else but loving her to the very edge of delirium and beyond. 'But I was the one who insisted we find out the truth so I can hardly complain now you have the bit properly between your teeth at last and refuse to let it go.'

'True, but I have to get dressed before I can find out if I'm right about where that letter is,' she said and looked about for the fine clothes they discarded with such delicious abandon as soon as the Dowager Lady Lathbury and Miss Lathbury departed for some fashionable crush until the small hours and left them the peace for their celebratory lovemaking.

Not that they had not celebrated a great deal in their intimately grand bedchamber and outside it whenever they had the chance. And she could hardly wait to make love with her husband with the terrible threat of discovery lifted off her shoulders, if she was right and that letter had been safe all along.

'If you think I'm going to lounge about the place naked as the day I was born like a kept man waiting on your pleasure, you are mistaken,' he said, reaching for his own lordly clothes and putting them on with a carelessness that would horrify his valet if he could see him, and even the idea made her stifle a giggle behind her hand at the thought of anyone seeing what they got up to behind closed doors, before or after they were married.

'Hmm, are you adding another trick to our fantasies, my lord?' she said with a teasing look that felt so good she nearly took all her clothes off again.

'Be quiet and get yourself dressed again, my lady, before I forget everything else and start playing out one of them right now,' he told her with a hot, driven look that said he wasn't entirely joking.

'We need to know for sure,' she said, serious again because they really did.

'Yes,' he said, and now she could see he was almost as apprehensive as she was under that lust and banter he had kept up to distract her. 'And hurry up,' he added as she tried to find a few hairpins so she could get her hair into some sort of order.

Of course, it didn't matter what the servants thought of them when they must have a very good idea Lord Lathbury was as tangled up in passion for her as their unexpected new lady was with him. 'I just feel as if I need to look sober and decent for this,' she explained.

'Then you will have failed on all counts, love,' he told her and scurried her upstairs for a very different reason than the one they were usually intent on lately.

'It won't matter if it's not there, Adam,' she told him very seriously as she opened the door to her boudoir and turned to face him very seriously indeed. 'You're right; I have to trust you will love me no matter what and protect my son from harm somehow even if it isn't where I think it is.'

'I will, but let's do this anyway. You will settle to being my lady better if you know one way or the other.'

'Very well,' she said and headed for the locked drawer of the elegant little writing desk in my lady's elegant boudoir. She held her breath as she opened it, reached for the book inside and turned back to face him so they could find this together.

He saw the unmistakable outline of a cross on its embossed cover, and she saw the light dawn in his eyes. 'A prayer book? Of course that's what she would call it if she was short of words to describe it to you and so desperate for you to know. Her book! The only one nobody else would think to touch or use unless she actually invited them to, and somehow I doubt if she ever did.'

'No, she always kept it by her bed, but managed to point from it to me often enough to make me understand she wanted me to have it, Adam. I didn't want to take it. I kept fooling myself she was better and would be able to use it again. Then it hurt too much to use it after she died. So I locked it away because it felt so personal it was wrong to use it instead of mine, and now I know why she was so restless until I told her I understood that she wanted me to have it. What an idiot I was not to have thought of it as soon as I read her last message.'

'You loved her and you were grieving; no wonder you didn't connect it to the book in her message.'

'No, it reminded me of her and that time too much to see it for what it is: her book.'

'Best let me do this, then,' he said, and he was so much gentler and wiser than most men; she supposed she owed that to his accident. He had had so many years to watch and observe his fellow human beings without being the centre of all the attention her once wild young lord must have accepted as his right. So much like her then, tucked away in her lair warily peering out at the world and not being part of it.

She snuggled under his arm and looked with him despite that kindness, her heart beating so fast she wondered if he could hear it or feel it because he was so attuned to her it sometimes felt as if they shared thoughts, let alone feelings.

He gently opened the finely wrought clasp that held the covers closed, and Melissa could see the familiar shuffle of papers inside it and tears pricked her eyes. There were a good many markers throughout the book and she could not go through them one by one and remember being next to her when her grandmother tucked that one in or tutted over that one and took it anyway.

'Shake them all out,' she said, and he looked at her. He must have seen how hard the waiting was for her and gently shook the fine old book over her little desk so that nothing could float to the floor and drift away for someone else to find. Then Adam laid the book down and went for more candles while Melissa swept all the dislodged papers into a heap and went through them page by page.

'It's not here,' she said at last. Try as she might to pretend it didn't matter, she heard the flat despair in her voice, and he must have, too.

'Of course it couldn't be that easy. Anyone might pick it up if she dropped it one day,' he said as if still trying to reason his way past her wildly fluctuating emotions. He picked up the finely made book and examined its endpapers carefully. 'Ah, there you are,' he said. 'Here's a split that's been so carefully sewn up again you can barely find it even when you know it's there. Here, feel it,' he invited and trailed her shaking index finger over the slight abrasion of a row of tiny stitches.

'I wish I was the sort who had fine needlework lying about now so I would have the right sort of scissors to hand.'

'I wouldn't let you near anything sharp when you are shaking like that,' he said half-seriously.

'You do it, then.'

He went into his dressing room for the finely honed razor his valet used to shave him however many times a day he felt the need to fight his dark whiskers for supremacy. Melissa felt the danger of the thing even as she watched Adam slice through those minute stitches and run the blade very carefully under the glue her grandparents must have applied to the gap for extra insurance. She knew they would have done this together, agreed to keep this paper safe for the boy's sake and not tell her. Adam handed her the single sheet of fine paper in her grandmother's tiniest handwriting, and Melissa realised she must have copied the original letter out before destroying it because this one was so much easier to hide.

'Grandmama made them promise to send her this letter saying where they were going to live a new life with my baby before she would hand him over, Adam, and to write again if they ever moved on or needed help,' she said with a wobble in her voice because here was the place her son was living and she didn't know if she could make herself stay away now she knew where he was. 'What am I to do now I have it, Adam?'

'Will you trust me to keep it safe since I don't think either of us can sew well enough to put it back where it came from?'

'I certainly can't and I doubt it's on a list of gentlemanly accomplishments you were taught as a boy. Can we let them know my grandmother is dead and their promise must come to me now, Adam?'

'It certainly has to be done somehow, but let's talk to your father about it in the morning, since he's a wily politician and might see a way to keep it secret while persuading them you need to see your boy now and again, even if it has to be from a distance.'

'Oh, Adam, do you really think I could?' she whispered, awed and shaken by hope she could lay eyes on him somehow to make sure he was safe and happy without her.

'I think you need to. I hope they understand that, and maybe we had better resurrect that wig since I never saw colouring like yours until I met you and you did say he shares it. But for now let's just get you to bed, my love. You look weary half to death after all this excitement and my masterly attentions.'

'And you're so modest with it,' she murmured as those attentions and the release of all that tension caught up with her and he lifted her into his arms. 'I do love you,' she told him sleepily when they were undressed again and in their marital bed to only sleep for once. There was no need to wait for him to say it back when he made it obvious in so many ways, so she slipped off into dreamland in his arms, and where else would she ever want to be when she did that?

Chapter Nineteen

'Are you sure you are ready to do this, Mel?' the Duke of Wiston asked his daughter with a concerned look six months later.

'Of course she can. My lady can do anything she sets her mind to,' Adam told his father-in-law with a frown he thought she couldn't see, and of course he was being even more protective and bearlike than usual today.

Not only was she about to meet her son for the first time in nearly eleven years, but she was already big with his unborn half-brother or -sister. At least Andrew Robert McFarlane's parents would be able to see their unlikely visitor was hardly likely to snatch her first child back when she was working so hard on her next one. Although they could be wrong about that, she decided as the fierce love she felt for her son the instant he came into the world rose up to remind her how desperately she had missed him all these years.

She hesitated and wondered if Adam's faith in her was misplaced.

'Go,' he said with a gentle push to set her in motion, and she wanted to cling to him so badly it felt as if her feet might sprout roots and hold her in place here with him, however much the rest of her wanted to join her father in the waiting carriage and see her son again for the first time in so terribly long.

'I wish you could come with us,' she said as him being missing from it threatened to take some of the bittersweet joy out of this meeting.

'My wife might have something very sharp to say if I was seen squiring a golden-haired, noticeably enceinte female about without her,' he told her with his best piratical grin to make light of it. 'You know I'm too distinctive to hide who I am from anyone who has heard about my scars and limping gait, my darling. You father is much easier to disguise than I am, and I think I trust him to keep you safe and out of mischief so long as you don't stay away for too long.'

'Not when some other yellow-haired strumpet might get her hooks in you while my back's turned,' she said as lightly as she could with all these butterflies and his baby in her belly.

She made herself leave and not look back as the hired carriage left the nearest large town to the McFarlanes' home. If she did, she might be too much of a coward to go on with this without him. No, she could do this; she was ready for the few precious moments she was to be granted in order to see for herself that her boy was indeed his parents' beloved, mischievous only child and perfectly safe in their care.

Adam was trying so hard not to fuss over her and he had not murmured more than a dozen times a day about the folly of her travelling even as slowly as they had got here during pregnancy. She needed to do this before their child was born because then she would soon have a baby to feed and care for and Adam to convince they would not break if he breathed on them the wrong way.

Thank heaven Andrew's parents had agreed to let her see him after she promised to pretend she was just a distant family connection and not make a great fuss of him. Somehow she would keep that promise, and she only had to picture Joe at the same age as their son was now to realise how hideous it would be for him if she wept all over him.

After an hour in a not very well-sprung hired carriage and ten minutes waiting in the chill November wind for the McFarlanes' coach to come and pick them up at the crossroads, so nobody knew exactly how they had got there, she was glad of the heavy cloak and cashmere shawls Adam had insisted on wrapping her up in. Then they were finally on their way and she could see what a fine country this was for a boy to grow up in. His parents' house looked like a home, and somehow she thought Joe would approve of their son growing up amid fine farmland and rolling hills.

She smiled at the thought of all the adventures

they used to have when they were supposed to be tucked up in their beds on early summer mornings and dark winter nights. At last she could look back on those times without the almost bottomless sea of grief she had been lost in for so long. She did still love her first love, but nowadays she could do it with a much lighter heart because she loved Adam so much as well. He had given her back her joy in life and the freedom to be her true self. At last he believed her when she said he was most definitely not hideous, and he seemed to have put his terrible guilt about the accident behind him.

Her smile at the thought of him pacing their hired parlour while she was gone went a little crooked because she knew what an effort it had cost him to come this far from home, then stay behind at the inn when he was right—he was much too distinctive to fade into the furniture. Her son would be fascinated by him where a fat lady in spectacles and a duke in disguise were hardly worth a second glance.

'So, how did you get on, then?' Adam asked his newly restored-to-herself wife after she put off her disguise.

'It was good.'

'Just good?'

'Yes, good enough. You can stop worrying; I don't have any plans to wrest him from his home and gallop away. He is everything I wanted him to be. His parents dote on him yet he isn't spoilt, and I fear they may be better at being one than I am likely to be.'

'You will be the best mother there is,' he argued and laid his hand on her pregnant belly as if he wanted her to feel how much he loved her and their coming child. 'The first time I saw you I thought you looked like a lioness, and I know you would have marched into hell to protect your cub, so don't you dare belittle yourself because you were forced to let him go.'

'I wish it could have been otherwise, of course I do. He and Joe were everything to me at the time but, oh, how dearly I love you now, Adam. I missed you so much today. Papa tries his hardest to make up for what we had to do to stop my baby being mocked and denigrated and fatherless. We understand one another so much better now, but he isn't you.'

'Well, no, he definitely isn't an ugly old bear who could not accompany his wife on one of the most important visits you are ever going to make.'

'Neither are you, and I thought I told you to stop feeling sorry for yourself.'

'Only when my ugly bearness gets in the way of being your husband, my lady.'

'Well, that's an improvement then. Does it stop you being one to your wife right now, my love?' she asked as she snuggled into his arms, and of course her father had had the tact to stay away while they discussed her day so they could sit here together by the fire and she could feel Adam's strength and support and simply relax with him after such a strange, longed-for day.

'Yes, you just drove over hard roads in a poorly

sprung carriage and did far more than I ever want you to do again in your condition, Lady Lathbury.'

'You're probably right, but I promise you I am not in the least bit tired.'

'Well, I am, so just be quiet and behave yourself or I will tell you about the fast baggage I met this spring who went about in breeches and burgled a respectable scholar's libraries without so much as a *By your leave, sir.*'

'She sounds exactly the sort of female a respectable scholar like you ought to avoid.'

'No, she is exactly the sort I needed to force me out of my lair and show me what I was missing, but are you sure you're all right, love?' he added as if he knew she was trying hard to come to terms with her old hurts and this new reality.

'Yes, he's such a fine boy, Adam, and I'm proud of him. He's more like Joe and a bit less like me than he was when he was born. His hair has darkened to chestnut and his face is more like Joe's than mine now. His eyes are still from me, though, so it's as well I put on those spectacles so he could not see them. He just dismissed me as some strange connection of his mother's and could not wait to be off and doing something more interesting.'

'That's fair enough since you looked like a quiz with them on as well as that hideous wig, my darling,' he teased as if he thought she needed distracting, but oddly enough she did not.

'We will not put them in our dressing-up box then; the children can have them,' she said comfortably, and for the first time she found she could talk about the family they were going to make together, God willing, and not feel a constant splinter of regret that her first-born son would never be a part of it. Andrew Robert McFarlane had his own family, a fine home and friends he had been restless to get back to as soon as he could escape the drawing room and a pair of odd strangers he would forget as soon as he was free to resume whatever mischief their arrival had interrupted.

'He is just a healthy and happy boy, Adam. I must leave him to carry on being who he is now, and that is Mr and Mrs McFarlane's son and not mine.'

'That's all well and good, but I know you still want him with you to fuss over deep down. You are a lioness indeed to let him go then and now, my darling.'

'I know, I'm a paragon,' she said with a self-mocking smile.

'Hardly,' he argued, 'you are a housebreaker and a hoyden and the love of my life, but you're certainly not one of those.'

'True.'

'At last, I thought they were never going to let me back into my own bedchamber again, my darling,' Adam said shakily and as if he had been striding up and down out in the corridor all night. She could believe it from the wild look of him when he was limping far more than he usually did nowadays.

'Are you quite worn out with pacing, my darling?' she asked with a tired smile.

'Says the woman who has just been through endless hours of hellish pain to bring my child into the world,' he told her as if he was almost at the end of his tether about the whole business of birth and being kept away from her when he desperately wanted to be here.

'You would have been no use at all and constantly ordering someone to do something to stop it or make things quicker and easier when they were busy enough already,' she told him. She was so weary, yet so full of love for this man and their new baby.

'Just look at him, Adam,' she urged as he seemed unwilling to take his eyes off her long enough to concentrate on their son. 'He's the image of you,' she added with a tender smile at the tiny baby tucked into the crook of her arm and never mind tiredness, she hadn't been able to let him go yet.

'What, eyepatch and limp and all?' her Adam asked with a smile past the tears in his eyes he undoubtedly thought were unmanly, the wonderful great fool.

'No, he's not that handsome yet, but he has your wild black hair and dark velvet eyes and a very lordly determination to get his own way,' she said, and all the fear she had lived with ever since she realised she was with child by him and might never love another child as she loved her first-born had faded the moment they laid Adam's son in her arms. She thought she already knew about motherhood, but she discovered love for her children didn't need to be shared out in slices because there was so much of it to go around.

'Currently I have a very lordly determination to make sure we sleep a mile apart every night and I will ride over to join you again here every morning, my love. There doesn't seem to be any other way to make sure I can keep my hands off you, and you need never go through that ordeal again.'

'There probably isn't one for us, and if you ride away from me every night I shall only come after you. Although I shall have to wait until I can endure being on a horse again to love you in every sense of the word, but then I'll be after you as fast as its legs can carry me. You are never getting away from me and the large family we can fit into the next however many years I have left to have them in if we try hard enough, my lord.'

'Spare me that terrifying prospect for tonight at least, Mel. I haven't got over the ordeal of this young gentleman's arrival yet, never mind thinking about the myriad brothers and sisters you are planning to inflict on him.'

'Hold him, Adam,' she said as she saw fear and acceptance in his eyes that he was going to have to go through this again because she was determined not to stop at two. 'He won't break,' she said tenderly as her husband looked down at their baby son as if he could hardly believe he was real and not breakable. 'I love you so much, Adam,' she said shakily. 'Joe gave me my first miracle, but you have given me yourself and another one when I thought I was going to be alone for the rest of my days.'

'I'm nobody's miracle,' he argued gruffly.

'You're mine, and stop arguing with me in my fragile state.'

'What, you're feeling fragile?' he barked with acute anxiety back in his gaze.

'I don't feel like a ten-mile hike or even getting out of bed just yet, but I soon will, so stop fussing and meet your first-born son properly.'

'My son,' he said and swallowed hard as their little boy began to stir and think about having a cry for food as he screwed up his face and shot out a tiny little fist to thump the air.

'Hold him while I sit up,' Melissa said and tried hard not to remember how different her life was the first time she felt her baby search for milk, then latch on to her as if he knew exactly what he needed to do to grow into a fine, strong boy. 'It's all right, he's just hungry again,' she said as Adam held their son out as if he would break and seemed at a loss to know how to comfort him, and he would be, wouldn't he? He lacked her experience of newborn sons as well as the necessary equipment to do something about it.

'Greedy little devil, isn't he?' Adam said as he watched his boy suckle at her breast with a mix of wonderment and pride and surprise.

'Just like his father,' Melissa said softly and stroked her baby's dark hair. Despite the pain and effort of childbirth she felt so content it was almost impossible to believe she had been so certain love could never happen twice in a lifetime and she would live her life alone for ever after giving up her first child. But it had. Here was the proof of it, her husband and their first child, and both of them all the more precious for being so unexpected and so very unlikely until she stole into Lathbury House one dark night and met her fate.

* * * * *

If you enjoyed this book, why not check out these other great reads by Elizabeth Beacon?

A Wedding for the Scandalous Heiress
A Rake to the Rescue
The Duchess's Secret
Marrying for Love or Money?
Unsuitable Bride for a Viscount
The Governess's Secret Longing